Love is
a time of enchantment:
in it all days are fair and all fields
green. Youth is blest by it,
old age made benign:
the eyes of love see
roses blooming in December,
and sunshine through rain. Verily
is the time of true-love
a time of enchantment — and
Oh! how eager is woman
to be bewitched!

SOMEONE WHO CARES

All Helen's romances seemed to peter out because the men concerned would demand too much too quickly, and Helen was old-fashioned enough to believe in love and marriage. Dared she hope that this time, with Micky, it would be different? Helen was half in love with him when he took her on holiday. Then, stranded because Micky had forgotten to refill her car's petrol tank, Helen met Shadrack . . . and he certainly was 'different'. Had she at last met someone who cared?

Books by Leslie Lance
in the Ulverscroft Large Print Series:

NURSE VERENA AT WEIRWATER

LESLIE LANCE

SOMEONE WHO CARES

Complete and Unabridged

ULVERSCROFT
Leicester

First published in Great Britain

First Large Print Edition
published December 1995

British Library CIP Data

Lance, Leslie
    Someone who cares.—Large print ed.—
Ulverscroft large print series: romance
I. Title
823.914 [F]

ISBN 0-7089-3432-3

Published by
F. A. Thorpe (Publishing) Ltd.
Anstey, Leicestershire
Set by Words & Graphics Ltd.
Anstey, Leicestershire
Printed and bound in Great Britain by
T. J. Press (Padstow) Ltd., Padstow, Cornwall

This book is printed on acid-free paper

To my dear friend,
IRENE ROBERTS,
who would certainly
have adopted 'Perkin'.

1

"I'VE behaved like an idiot!" I groaned. "I should have waited till the morning."

On the passenger's seat beside me, the fluffy black-and-white pup gave a whimper, as if of assent.

"You needn't moan. You're jolly lucky," I told him. "I might have left you behind — and then what would have happened to you? They wouldn't have fed you. Greta said it was wrong of me to rescue you and fuss over an abandoned puppy, when there are so many starving children in the world. That's the way she talks, and I suppose she believes what she says, but she can't even provide a decent meal for that precious commune, except from poached game and pinched tins."

Anger was leaping up in me again. I had had to speak my mind. How could I have waited? Granted, it was a foul night, with drenching icy rain and fearsome gusts of wind, and a deepening sea-mist.

Visibility, in the gathering darkness, was becoming severely restricted. The small Peugeot's wipers, normally most efficient, could scarcely cope with this torrential rain, and the windows were misting over inside the car.

Not at all the right weather conditions for an heroic gesture, for storming out and wiping the cloying greyish mud of the Down to Earth commune from my gum-boots; but I hadn't paused to consider that. I had been carried away by my fiery indignation.

"Down to Earth, indeed! Living off the land? You're not a commune. You're just a den of petty thieves," I had exploded. "Crime is crime, and no doubt some of you can find arguments in its favour . . . protests against Society and the established order . . . a way of making your voice heard and your opinions taken seriously . . . a means of taxing those who have waxed fat by exploiting workers or consumers. Oh, I've heard it all, ad nauseam, but nothing you say can excuse the utterly contemptible things you do! Filching tins from a wretched, short-sighted, innocently trusting old woman in a village Post Office and Stores! How can you stoop so low?"

"Steady now, Curly! You don't have to get all hot under the collar on Mrs Hickson's account. She's no soul of honesty. She has added at least twopence on the supermarket prices of her goods," Robin had interposed pacifically. "In some cases, she has added as much as fivepence. She's exploiting tourists and holiday-makers."

"She's offering them a service. She's also saving them petrol. One gallon of petrol costs considerably more than a few extra pence," I had pointed out. "Besides, she can't afford to order tins in the quantities the supermarkets do, so she has to pay more for them."

"She charges twelvepence more for that fancy souvenir soap," Greta had observed disapprovingly. "It's rubbishy stuff, at that. I don't know why you're het up about that old fraud, Curly. With her 'loves' and 'ducks' and smarmy smiles, she's quite nauseating."

"Whatever she is or isn't, you've no excuse for robbing her," I had flashed. "And my name's Helen — as I have repeatedly told you."

"Helen! Helen of Troy or Sweet Nell of Old Drury?" pony-tailed, sallow, sharp-featured Lettice, nicknamed Cos, had scoffed. "Why cling to a hopelessly outmoded name?"

"It happens to be mine."

"No need to make an issue of it," Micky had drawled. "Calm down, Copper-Knob. You're a guest here, remember?"

That had been the final, irrevocable blow. I had stared dazedly at his handsome, mocking face, and, perhaps for the first time, had seen the icy coldness of his brilliant blue eyes. I had seen — or forced myself to recognise — other things about him, too; things which I had been discovering ever since the start of this ill-fated 'holiday'.

In Plymouth, meeting Micky for odd dates, on my free evenings or at weekends, I had been stupidly bemused by the look of him, and the lazy, off-beat charm he knew so well how to exert. Those clear-cut features, that smooth, short fair hair, and clean, freshly shaven look, together with his good, casually

4

elegant clothes, had attracted me instantly and strongly. Micky had seemed such a delightful and striking contrast to the general scruffiness, the beards and the shoulder-length hair, the grimy jeans and cheap anoraks of the other lads who had pressed me for dates. I had gone out with a few of them through sheer desperation. Evenings spent all alone in a strange city could seem intolerably long. I had tried to swallow my resentment of their 'take it or leave it' manner, their absurd, unjustified swaggering, the cheap eating places, reeking of hot cooking fat and onions, to which they had taken me for a 'snack', and their clumsy fumblings under the table.

All those dates had ended awkwardly, if not with actual unpleasantness. So — I was a prude, a snob, a frigid virgin — or something worse? Could I help it? I was the product of my birth and upbringing. My mother was a busy, dedicated country doctor. My father was a country vicar, with two churches and a scattered flock. They were both kindly, hard-working, lovable and loving. I was their only offspring and they had struggled painstakingly not to be possessive over me.

Perhaps it was because they had deliberately left me free to live my own life and reach my own decisions that I had never been in revolt against their standards. I wasn't a natural kicker over of traces. I loved a quiet and orderly and useful existence. I had trained as a children's nurse and found congenial work with 'Kiddy-Care' . . . 'By those who really care for kiddies', as the advertisements put it.

'Kiddy-Care' specialised in providing a temporary child-minding service. Mothers in desperate need of a holiday, or recently-made-widower fathers, could safely hand over a whole family to a 'Kiddy-Care' nurse.

Some assignments were inevitably more rewarding and less exacting than others, but on the whole I had enjoyed my various posts . . . until the last one.

"Three small girls, father abroad, mother expecting a fourth baby," I had been briefed. "Well-to-do people. Father's a company director. Mother's studying for a degree. Cook, gardener, and daily help employed. Pleasant, modern house, a few miles from Plymouth. Should be right up your street, Helen. The children have ponies, and you can ride, can't you?"

Oh, yes, I could ride! I had most of the qualifications of a girl who had grown up in the depths of the country. I was an excellent walker, and I could drive — a horse or a car. I could bottle or freeze fruit, make jams and marmalades, grow, cook and prepare vegetables for the deep freeze. I could distinguish unerringly between mushrooms and other varieties of edible fungi, and those commonly known as 'toadstools' which were poisonous. That knowledge, incidentally, had been one of Micky's selling points when he had introduced me to the Down to Earth crowd.

"This is Helen. She knows all about fungi and herbs, and weeds one can eat," he had announced. "She'll save us a lot of money on the catering. I'll bet she's a good cook, too . . . "

I wasn't. Cooking was my mother's hobby and pet form of relaxation, so I hadn't had much experience in our vicarage kitchen. I could cook a reasonably good meal when necessary, but cooking wasn't my thing, and I had no intention of constituting myself general cook to this odd-looking assembly. That would be anything but the holiday Micky had promised me.

"Fresh sea air, a delightful site, and a jolly good crowd of worth-while people," he had enthused. "You'll be in your element, Curly."

Yes, I who professed to loathe nicknames, had let Micky Harris call me 'Curly', without more than a token protest. I had been almost wholly under his spell on that Saturday morning when I had collected him and his suitcase on Plymouth Hoe.

"No point in taking two cars. Energy conservation," he had said easily. "The Down to Earthers are against mechanical means of transport, which use oil and petrol and pollute the air."

"They sound a bit cranky," I had said doubtfully. "I may be a misfit there. I'm not a good mixer . . . a herd person."

"You don't know that. You haven't tried. They'll love you, and you'll take to the life like a duck to the water,"

8

Micky had prophesied, with a sad lack of originality.

Outwardly, he had struck me as marvellously distinctive; a genuine individualist, who dared to stick to his own style. It came as a mild shock to listen to the stock phrases and hackneyed opinions and time-worn compliments which flowed so eloquently from his well-cut lips.

The seeds of disillusionment must have been there, from the very first, but I had been determined not to let them germinate. The sad truth was that I was willing myself to fall in love with Micky. I hadn't had a real love-affair since my 'teens — and now I was twenty-four. I was old-fashioned enough to yearn for a husband, a home, and children of my own. I believed in marriage, 'for better for worse . . . in poverty and in riches. cleave thee only unto him . . . ' and all those solemn promises. I found freedom a lonely mode of existence. I wanted to be tied down, by secure and lasting bonds.

Perhaps, had I made my views clear to Micky early on in our acquaintanceship, he would swiftly have dropped me, but I didn't. I chose to fool myself that he felt the same way. Looking back over our dates, I was convinced that he had deliberately encouraged me to believe that he was in dead earnest. He had that kind of sincere yet beguiling manner which could make his listeners believe almost any fallacy. It was, of course, part of his stock in trade as a 'confidence man' . . . but I had never met a confidence trickster before. How could I have been expected to recognise one?

Perhaps the seeds of distrust had begun to germinate on that hundred miles' drive up to Dorset, Certainly, they had burst through their outer coating when he had introduced me to the commune.

Owing to Micky's insistence on a number of detours — "to show you the countryside" — it had been dusk when we had arrived at the encampment, and most of the residents had been gathered round a traditional camp-fire, with an iron pot steaming over it. They had eyed me as if I were a visitor from outer space. I had gazed back at them in dawning dismay.

I must subconsciously have expected the commune to be on the lines of a kibbutz. I hadn't been prepared for the haphazard, gipsyish layout of weather-worn caravans, sagging tents, and roughly constructed cabins of boards and galvanised iron, backed by one substantial old stone barn, its slated roof patched in places by pieces of rusting galvanised iron. There were cobbles in front of the barn, muddy now but still preferable to the surrounding, trampled grass. It was on the cobbles that the camp fire had been built.

The barn, I learned later, belonged to Greta and her husband, Jacko, who had founded the commune. He was a potter and she was a weaver. The barn was both their dwelling-house and their studio. They were an earnest, humourless couple, who honestly believed they were founding a new order. They tried hard to credit others with their own sincerity. They were patently loth to admit what registered on me in my first horrified glance, that half the company consisted of layabouts and drop-outs, who regarded 'work' as a dirty word.

Even Micky's hand, resting affectionately and possessively on my shoulder, couldn't ease my embarrassment and disquietude as I stood there, being assessed by suspicious, hostile, or leering eyes.

Greta, peering at me through thick-lensed, black rimmed glasses had said doubtfully: "Well, welcome, Helen! You don't look quite the type, but if Micky is sponsoring you . . . "

"Wherever did you find her, Micky? In a confectioner's?" Barbara, plump and spotty and vacuous looking, and generally known as Booby, had giggled. "Isn't she a pretty thing? Can she walk and talk?"

I had soon discovered that 'pretty' and 'nice' were terms of opprobrium to most of the crowd; at least to the female portion! Men, even hippy types, were rarely blind to feminine attractions.

Nature had designed me — the child of two undeniably handsome parents — as 'a pretty girl', and I saw no reason to attempt to frustrate her design. I had riotously curling, darkly red hair, darkly brown eyes, a pleasingly shaped nose, upward curving lips, a firmly moulded

12

chin, a peaches-and-cream skin, and a lithe, trim figure.

"Nothing to be conceited about, my dear child. You just happen to be lucky in your looks," Mother had told me repeatedly. "Make the most of your assets, but don't attach too much importance to them. It's what you *are* which matters . . . "

"Pay no attention to this young woman, Curly. She's merely envious," Micky had said, squeezing my shoulder. "Booby knows she'd have to lose at least twenty pounds and all her many spots before she could be considered appetising."

That had been the first time I had been made reluctantly conscious of the streak of cruelty in Micky. The wretched Booby had turned an ugly, beetroot crimson beneath her acne, and some of the other girls had sniggered.

"Appetising," the thin, sallow-faced, bespectacled youth later introduced to me as 'Robin' — surnames were rarely used here — had echoed reflectively. "I guess so. If you go for models who look as if they've just emerged from a beauty salon."

"Is she a model?" Greta had inquired, with an ominous frown.

"Certainly not. I'm a nurse . . . " I had found my voice at last. "If I'm not welcome here, I don't have to stay."

"You're welcome. Any friend of Micky's is welcome," Greta's thick-set, heavily bearded husband had interposed. "Sit down, girl! It's feeding time."

The stew had been surprisingly good, if a somewhat odd mixture. I had detected pieces of pheasant among the more solid lumps of pork and chicken, with cauliflower, potato, and carrots, and a flavouring of cider. This was the second weekend in October, I remembered, but, even so, pheasant came into the category of luxury foods.

Involuntarily, I had said so, and there had been an awkward silence, until a foxy-faced man had said airily: "Living off the land, aren't we? And the woods around here are swarming with pheasants. Sally forth at night with a torch and a stout stick and Bob's your uncle."

"Foxy's Dad is gamekeeper on a big estate. Foxy knows all the tricks," the sharp-featured 'Cos', close beside him

14

had piped up admiringly.

"Your Dad's estate, isn't it?" Micky had hinted, and the girl had glowered at him.

She was the Honourable Lettice Somebody, Micky had told me later; a drop-out from an Oxford college; only he had used the word 'escapee' instead of 'drop-out'.

An oddly assorted crowd, indeed; high on freedom and self-expression, but low — or it seemed to me — on achievement. That first evening, I was irritated and bewildered and utterly at a loss. I could not see what Micky could have in common with such a bunch. Unless I was all wrong about him, he was ambitious and a worker, with a keen eye to material advantages and possessions. He wore a £150 wrist-watch and his clothes hadn't been bought off the peg. He had told me, rather vaguely, that he was an 'agent'. I wasn't sure what that meant, but he hadn't encouraged me to probe.

"I'm a go-between. I help to fix deals between interested parties. Needs a keen ear and eye and lashings of tact. Tricky at times, but profitable," he had answered casually. "And — I'm my own master."

It had been quickly apparent that Micky was immensely popular with most of the commune's members. Even Greta, who evidently regarded him as a back-slider, and not what she called 'fully committed', had an indulgent, elder-sisterly attitude towards him. Probably, some of the menfolk were jealous of Micky and his obvious assets, but most of the girls clustered round him.

It had been equally apparent that these friends of his could not imagine what he saw in *me*. That was especially plain when they discovered that I had no intention of sharing a tent with him. The girls were quite shocked. They clearly thought I was crazy not to seize such a grand opportunity. Micky himself, for once, had looked taken aback, but he had regained his customary poise with speed and good humour.

"Helen's new to this kind of scene. I don't propose to rush her," he had pronounced, with a tolerant, man of the world smile. "Anticipation whets the appetite . . . ."

16

"Give her a perch in the hen roost, and she'll soon change her mind," Jacko had grinned.

The 'hen roost' was a Felbur hut, arranged with bunk beds, somewhat after the fashion of a school dormitory. It was occupied by those female members who were — temporarily in most instances — without or between boy friends. The beds were hard, the amenities poor, and privacy virtually non-existent, but I had tried to conceal my dismay. I was spoilt and over-fastidious, I had told myself. Surely, for Micky's sake, I could endure these conditions for a few days? I ought to welcome new experiences . . . and I was in love with Micky, wasn't I?

Already, as I had hurriedly prepared for bed on that first evening, there had been a big black question mark in my mind. If I were truly in love, would I shrink from becoming wholly committed? Wouldn't I be ready to put aside the qualms and restrictions inherent in my upbringing? Was some sixth sense warning me to step back, before I plunged out of my depth and into a perilous current?

I had tossed and turned on that hard,

narrow bunk, trying desperately to analyse my own emotions. I hadn't reached any satisfactory conclusion. I would simply have to walk warily and wait, I had decided wearily.

I had lasted out a week, for which, I considered, I deserved some credit. I had not been guilty of the harsh, unfair and ill-considered judgment of which Greta had accused me. I had conceded that she and Jacko were sincere and well meaning, but I thought them either singularly short-sighted or else deliberately obtuse. As for their sense of values, it certainly wasn't mine and never would be. I reached out to pat the whimpering pup beside me . . .

There had been four pups in that feebly wriggling sack which, to my horror, I had spotted in the village pond. I had tried to hook the sack out by means of a stick, but had failed to reach it. Micky had tried to help me, but he had baulked at stepping into that slimy, muddy water. I had rolled my slacks up to my knees and floundered out through stinking mud and unidentified but horrid-feeling debris. The water had been over my knees before

I could grip the sack — and those slacks would never be the same again — but I had brought my burden triumphantly to the bank. Two of the pups had been beyond resuscitation, and the third had died that same day. The fourth, bathed and dried and fed, had perked up with commendable spirit and had attached himself firmly to me.

Greta had disapproved of my adopting him, and Micky hadn't been enthusiastic.

"The rule here is 'no pets', and what can you do with a dog, anyway? You can't hope to take him with you on assignments for Kiddy Care," he had reminded me.

"I'll work something out . . . or find a good home for him. I may not go back to Kiddy Care. I've been temporarily suspended, remember?" I had countered. "That's why I'm here."

It hadn't occurred to me not to be frank with Micky about my summary dismissal from my most recent assignment. He had appeared sympathetic and indignant on my behalf. He had insisted that I had earned a holiday.

I had broken one of Kiddy Care's

most stringent rules . . . "no corporal punishment in any circumstances", but not without some justification. Admittedly, I shouldn't have lost my temper with a nine-year-old, however infuriating, but the child in question had repeatedly scoffed at my admonitions. She was a competent rider for her age, and she had a beautiful, admirably schooled pony, on whom she had won quite a collection of cups and rosettes at gymkhanas. It had been one of my duties to drive the Land Rover, with the horse box behind it, and to shepherd young Caroline through the various events for which she had been entered.

She wasn't an endearing child. Already, she gave promise of being as conceited and petulant as her mother, who fancied herself as an intellectual married to a Philistine of a husband, and was deeply resentful of her fourth pregnancy. Caroline was loth to accept criticism or even advice. Blunders were always the pony's fault, rather than her own. I had had to rebuke her sharply on several occasions for using her whip unnecessarily and in ill humour.

At this particular show, she had sailed triumphantly through the first round, and had almost gone clear in the second. At the final triple fence, she had used her whip at precisely the wrong moment. The pony had reared, checked, and missed his stride. In spite of an heroic effort on his part, he had caught a hoof in the final fence . . . and Caroline had dropped into third place.

When I had reached her, she had been lashing and kicking the wretched pony unmercifully and calling him "a stupid beast".

"You're the stupid one — " I had flashed — and she had promptly lashed me across the throat.

I should, of course, have played it cool, but I'd had my fill of that spoilt young madam. I had lifted her off the pony and across my knee. I had administered half a dozen spanks before I had released her. By then, she had been sobbing — from rage rather than pain. I hadn't left any marks on her, as I had pointed out to her outraged mother. Perhaps not, but I had humiliated Caroline before her friends and so subjected her to a traumatic experience. There could be no foreseeing what deleterious effect such crude, violent handling would have on her personality, Mrs Forrester had reasoned angrily. I wasn't fit to have charge of a highly intelligent and sensitive child. 'Kiddy Care' should have known better than to employ such an uncontrolled and violent person. I must apologise to Caroline, pack my cases, and leave as soon as 'Kiddy Care' had provided a substitute.

I certainly would not apologise for administering the kind of discipline Caroline badly needed, I had retorted. I would pack and leave immediately — and waive a week's salary in lieu of notice. Mrs Forrester could tell 'Kiddy Care' what she pleased. I would make my own report to the firm.

The two younger children had wailed and wept when I had left, which had been some kind of compensation, but I had earned my first black mark from 'Kiddy Care'. The manageress, to whom I had spoken over the telephone, hadn't been entirely unsympathetic, but she had reminded me that the firm's reputation rested on a strict adherence to the printed rules. I had signed a contract, promising to observe those rules, no matter what the provocation.

She suggested that I should take a fortnight's leave on half-pay, and decide whether I could conform to the rules in future or not. Under the terms of the contract, I could be crossed off the books here and now, but she was reluctant to lose a good and hitherto satisfactory nurse. I had accepted her proposal, which I had considered entirely fair. I had needed just such a breathing space. Micky had become increasingly pressing and, though he hadn't actually mentioned marriage yet, I had fooled myself that he would before long.

A fortnight's holiday would give me time to decide whether I wanted to go on working for 'Kiddy Care', or whether I was going to marry Micky, I had reflected. As it had happened, I had known within a week that there could be no future for me with Micky Harris. On basic issues, we were fundamentally and irrevocably opposed. My outburst of furious indignation at the petty stealing from the village stores had merely brought about the inevitable end a week earlier. I might have found excuses for his refusal to condemn his friends' depredations. I couldn't forgive his betrayal of my confidence.

Lettice, nicknamed 'Cos', who had obviously resented my unvoiced but possibly obvious disapproval of her boy friend, Foxy, had unwittingly given Micky away.

"So high and mighty and self-righteous, aren't we?" she had derided me. "Turning up our nose at a bit of unofficial taxing of the exploiters! What's the odd poaching or pinching compared to violence and brutality?"

I must have gaped at her in blank non-comprehension. I hadn't had an inkling of her meaning.

"Looking so sweet and innocent! Who'd ever guess that you would thrash a small child till she screamed for mercy?" Lettice had elucidated. "We've heard all about it."

I had been shocked and speechless. I had looked at Micky — and he hadn't even coloured. He had gazed back at me blandly.

"Cos, as usual, exaggerates," he had drawled. "All the same, she has a point. Are you really in a position to throw stones?"

"To us, cruelty is the only major sin," Robin had added earnestly. "To terrorise a child is far worse than filching a few tins from an exploiter of the people."

"If you call a few well-deserved spanks 'cruelty', it's obviously futile to argue with you," I had got out at last. "I don't fit in here, and I never could. Thank you for your hospitality to date . . . and good-bye."

2

MICKY hadn't wanted me to leave. When I had stalked off to the hen roost, to repack the few belongings I had unpacked, he had followed me. He had been at his most eloquent . . . pleading, teasing, flattering, and seeking to beguile me again.

He had given me the whole treatment and I had reacted to it with stony silence. I was hurt and I was angry. I had to whip up my anger in order to conceal the hurt. Somehow, I had felt that I couldn't bear Micky to guess how nearly I had fallen wholeheartedly in love with him.

"Curly, can't you see? I had to give them all some good reason for your presence. As Greta said first off, you simply don't look the type. I had to explain that you had been thrown out of a job at a minute's notice."

"For brutality to a small child?"

"Oh, rats! Naturally, I didn't put it like that. Cos twists everything. You must have noticed that. Why did you let her get under your skin? Come on, now! Forget it . . . " He had put his arms round me then, as I had bent over my bulging suitcase, and drawn me close to him. "Curly, you can't walk out on me now. I won't have it . . . "

Given another few minutes of his practised charm, his deft touch, and his apparent penitence, would I have weakened? I couldn't be entirely certain. I had been spared the temptation by Booby . . . well-meaning, clumsy, blundering Booby. She had come bouncing into the hen roost, exclaiming volubly: "Oh, Helen, I'm so sorry you're going! You've been really nice to me, and I'd hoped we were going to be true friends. Must you go? Cos is a cat. I don't believe a word she says. I'm sure you weren't cruel. Look how you saved that miserable puppy!"

She had pulled up short, as Micky had swung round, scowling.

"Oh, sorry! I didn't realise you were here, Micky love. Can't you make her change her mind? Or — is it all off between you two?" she had floundered on naively. "You never stick to any girl for long, do you?"

Booby had been one of those who had resented me on my arrival, but during the past week her attitude had changed. She and I had occupied neighbouring bunks and she had waxed confidential after 'lights out'. I had listened, perforce, to her accounts of her unhappy home-life — a once-adored father and an unsympathetic young stepmother — her unhappy big romance — jilted just before the wedding day — and her failure to find a congenial job. She had been a shop assistant, a waitress, a washer-up in an hotel, and a ward maid in a hospital, but always something had gone wrong.

"I'm what they call a born loser," she had lamented. "I even tried to commit suicide once, by jumping into the river at home. That was a washout, too. There wasn't enough water at the time, and I got myself stuck in horrid, thick mud. I had to be hauled out by a rope, like a stranded pony."

It had been Robin who had introduced her to the Down to Earthers. She had a small allowance from her father, sufficient to pay for her 'board and lodging', she had told me. She was basically a kind-hearted, ingenuous character, always ready to tackle the less inviting chores, cheerfully if unskilfully. There hadn't been any 'really close relationship' between her and Robin, she had admitted regretfully, but she still hoped that there might be.

Booby was the nearest approach to a friend that I had made in the commune. It had seemed ironical that she had been the one to ensure my escape from it. She had hovered around, talking incessantly, while I had hurriedly completed my packing, then she had helped me to carry the cases to my car.

Micky had left the hen roost abruptly, after Booby had observed ingenuously: "We all thought you were really serious this time . . . but you're not the marrying kind, are you? And it's plain that Helen is. Well, why not? I mean to say a girl with her looks doesn't need to sleep around. She can afford to hold out for marriage."

Booby wasn't such a fool as most people thought her, I had realised. Micky had glared at her as if he would gladly have throttled her. Then, he'd swung on his heel.

"Where are you going? Keep in touch, won't you?" Booby had pleaded, giving me an affectionate hug. "Have you any money? I could lend you a fiver . . . "

"Sweet of you, but I have enough," I had reassured her. "I'll find somewhere. I can always go home . . . "

Except that my parents had at last achieved a cherished desire and gone on a packaged tour of the Holy Land, I had remembered belatedly, and a locum would be in residence at the Vicarage. No matter. Accommodation would be readily available at this time of year. Hotels might not accept the puppy, but there were plenty of caravan sites. A caravan — to myself — would seem like sheer luxury after the hen roost.

Time I found shelter for the night, I decided, as another squally gust shook my sturdy little car. I had wanted to put some mileage between me and the commune, in case Micky should decide to seek me out again. I'd only covered around twenty miles now, but darkness was descending early tonight. The sooner

I was settled in somewhere warm and dry, the better. A notice board showed up dimly through the curtain of rain.

'Heatherview Caravan Park', it announced. 'First class caravans for hire. Children and pets welcome'.

"Well, that'll be a pleasant change for us," I told the wriggling pup beside me.

An arrow was pointing up a side road. I turned off the main road — and the Peugeot's engine gave an apologetic cough — and died on me.

"Oh, no!" I said aloud, staring incredulously at the petrol gauge. "Oh, Micky!"

Only that morning, he had borrowed my car for some unspecified errand, and I had handed over a £5 note for petrol. He hadn't wanted me to accompany him. He'd talked vaguely of "business . . . boring but necessary . . . " and had taken Robin with him. The tank couldn't be empty, I thought feverishly. Micky couldn't just have pocketed my fiver. Why would he? Hadn't he plenty of money of his own?

I pressed the self-starter frantically. Out of petrol — on a night like this, and at a time when the roadside garages would inevitably be closed? Surely fate couldn't be that unkind? The engine fired and the car moved forward a few yards . . . only to stop again. How far away was the caravan park? I wondered desperately. I might be able to find help there. It was obviously my best bid. It would be futile to march along the road in this torrential rain, so late in the evening, in a search for a petrol pump. This was a lonely stretch of the coast. I hadn't passed a village for miles, but this side road must lead to a settlement of some kind.

Luckily there was a slight incline. I slid the gear into neutral and the car began to cruise forward slowly. Twice, I had to hop out and push, and then hurl myself back into the driver's seat as the car gathered momentum. We progressed like that for about half a mile. Then, to my relief, I spotted a board, swinging madly in the wind. I could just discern the heading 'Heatherview Caravan Park', and, below it, a concrete drive sloping downwards. Had the incline been upwards, I would have had to leave the car and investigate on foot. I should have spotted the rows of dark, silent caravans, and realised that the Park had been closed for the winter.

As it was, I headed the Peugeot thankfully down the drive and was only belatedly aware that there were no lights anywhere. By such comparatively trivial circumstances are our destinies decided. When the car came to rest on a small plateau, and I perceived that the caravans surrounding it were unlighted and deserted, it was too late to turn back. I could not possibly push the car up that quite steep incline to regain the road.

When I switched off the engine and stepped out into the rain again, I was instantly conscious of the silence. It seemed to blanket the site like the gathering darkness. It was punctuated only by the creak of the swinging notice board at the head of the drive, a suggestion of waves on a not-too-distant shore, and a spasmodic harsh flapping, as of a loose sheet of galvanised iron.

I retrieved my torch from the car's pigeonhole and pressed the switch, but it was only a pocket torch, and its beam merely illuminated the white, ghostly looking shapes of the nearby caravans. I swung it this way and that — and saw muddy tracks leading in different directions from the plateau. One must lead to an office, a headquarters of some kind, even to a house, supposing the proprietor lived on the site, I thought hopefully. One — but which? The rain had lessened, but the wind was still at near gale force, and a thick mist hung over what I took to be the coast-line.

As I paused, a light suddenly appeared from somewhere among the massed caravans. It was being swung this way and that as though searching for someone or something. I raised my torch and waved it. Instantly, the other more powerful beam steadied and advanced towards me.

"Hello, there!" a man's voice called. "Who's that?"

It wasn't precisely an aggressive demand, but it held a curious mixture of caution and impatience. It was as though the caller expected the answer to come from an importunate friend whom he would have preferred to ignore.

"Hello!" I called back. "I'm stranded."

"Stranded?"

He came up fast, almost at a run. The torch beam was directed straight at me. My much feebler light showed me a stocky figure in anorak, jeans and gumboots . . . a completely anomymous figure. I supposed I must look almost equally anonymous to him, in my fawn mackintosh and brown trouser suit, with a scarf over my hair.

"What are you doing here? The camp's closed," he said, the impatience more pronounced.

"I didn't realise that. I saw the board and I wanted accommodation, at least for the night."

"Sorry, sister! You're out of luck. Try the village."

"I can't, I'm out of petrol," I said flatly. "Unless you've a spare can, I'm stuck here. Surely you can let me have one of the caravans." I was afraid he might jump to the conclusion that I was trying a hard-luck story on him. Something in his tone and the way he was directing the torch on me indicated that he was sceptical of my bona-fides, so I added hastily: "I'm all right. I mean, I can pay for the caravan."

"Can you?" He sounded openly sceptical now. "Fifty quid a week — payable in advance?"

"That's all right. Unless you've some petrol — "

"I haven't. The camp and shop are closed. I'm just here to check up and see everything is battened down," he said shortly. "I don't own the place. My uncle does. He's up country at the moment."

"You could let me have one of the caravans, couldn't you? I'd leave it clean and tidy," I said desperately.

"You'd stay here all alone, on a deserted site?"

"I wouldn't mind being alone."

It would be bliss after the stuffy, over-crowded hen roost, I thought, trying the effect of a propitiatory smile. Micky had told me once that my smile could melt icicles. He'd added that it had a touching innocence about it, which rightfully belonged to a four-year-old rather than to a grown woman.

Certainly, it seemed to work on my interlocutor. He lowered the torch-beam and shrugged his shoulders.

"O.K., then! If you're willing to pay in advance, I guess you can't do any harm here. You don't look like a window basher," he conceded. "No boy friend lurking in the background?"

"None. I'm — I'm a children's nurse on holiday. My name's Helen Melville."

"Right, then, Helen!" he responded briskly. "Car's stuck? Well, it's out of the way here. I'll fetch you some juice in the morning."

"That would be very kind of you," I said gratefully.

"Get your gear together while I open up a caravan for you. Further in will be best, where the light won't be seen from the road. Mustn't give passers-by the impression that the camp's still open."

"Anywhere that's dry will do."

He had a point about the light. Should Micky by any chance have decided to follow me, I would prefer to be as inconspicuous as possible.

I turned back to the car. I tucked the whimpering pup under my raincoat and retrieved my overnight case from the boot. The man in charge hadn't waited to give me a hand. Chivalry was a dead word these days, I thought regretfully, as, burdened by the suitcase, the wriggling pup, my handbag and torch, I floundered after the retreating beam of light. Once off the concrete of the drive, the ground was soggy and slippery.

My friend-in-need had halted midway up what appeared to be the centre of the massed caravans. He had tucked his torch under his arm and was fiddling with the lock of the caravan when I caught up with him.

"Having trouble?" I asked, and his sturdy shoulders twitched impatiently.

"Can't unlock the office tonight to find the right key. This key is supposed to fit most of the locks," he jerked out — and stepped down, to move on to the next caravan. A few more twiddles, and he said triumphantly: "Here we are, sister! I'll bring you the key along tomorrow. O.K.?"

I would have liked to have had the key tonight, but it would be ungracious as well as unwise to quibble, so I said: "Thank you. Thank you very much."

"There's still a cylinder, and, with any luck, you'll find some Calor gas left in it," he informed me. "Got matches?"

"Somewhere . . . "

I put down my suitcase and opened my handbag. The puppy was squirming against me. My torch jerked upward and momentarily illuminated a swarthy face, framed in the anorak's hood. He had ensured that no hair was visible except a pair of bushy dark eyebrows. They drew together in a scowl as their owner ducked back hastily. Had I inadvertently shone the torch in his eyes?

"Sorry!" I said absently. "Yes, I've matches here."

"What's that under your coat?" he demanded on a suspicious note. "Baby?"

"Dog, not human. A stray pup."

"Can you keep him quiet? A barking dog . . . "

"He's not really old enough to bark. Anyway, there's not anybody here for him to disturb, is there?"

"Neighbours down the road. A dog barking would make them wonder . . . "

"Would that matter?" I asked innocently.

"You never know . . . " came the evasive answer. "Against rules to open up the place again — and old Westcott's a stickler for the rules. No point in asking for trouble."

"Old Westcott?" I nearly said: "I thought the owner was your uncle," but I checked myself. Micky had told me that I had "an irritating tendency to pose tactless questions". I certainly didn't want to irritate this friend in need.

He was holding out his right hand. I would have put the box of matches into it, but he jerked his hand back in another impatient gesture.

"The dough, sister! Payment in advance," he reminded me.

"Oh, of course! Sorry! Will a cheque do? I have a Banker's card."

"No way. This is a cash deal."

"Between you and me?" I surmised. "Nothing to do with Uncle?"

"Sharp, aren't you? What Uncle doesn't know won't give him any headaches."

"I suppose not. I'll have to see how much I have left in my suitcase. I've only a pound or two in my purse."

"Get cracking, then! I can't hang around here half the night."

He certainly wasn't high on chivalry. He was sounding as if he would like to shake me. Definitely disgruntled. Not an exactly pleasant or endearing character. Just my luck. If I were as much a ready-made heroine of romance as, according to Micky, I looked, I would have been befriended by a tall, dark, handsome hero type, who would have fallen for me on sight. A breathtaking interlude would have followed, in which I should have swiftly forgotten all about Micky Harris.

I struggled up the steps into the caravan and thankfully put the pup down. My suitcase was handed up to me in a dour silence. With fingers which seemed to have become cramped and stiff, I searched my handbag for the little key. Then, with the pup nuzzling my ankles, I knelt down to unlock the case and rummage for my wallet.

I didn't habitually carry much cash around with me, but Micky had warned me that the commune was some distance from the nearest town and banks. He had advised me to bring my spending money in notes. I had three £10 notes and four fivers left, I discovered.

"I'll give you £40 now and the other

£10 later," I said firmly. "I must keep some cash back for food and petrol."

"No need. I'll bring you a five-gallon tin of petrol come morning," he assured me. "Don't try to welsh on our deal! It won't pay you."

There was the unpleasant hint of a threat in that. I swallowed down my rising indignation and passed over the remaining two fivers. I must have petrol. With a replenished tank, I could head for Bridport and change a cheque, I reminded myself.

"Right, then! Keep a low profile, as they say, and have a good holiday," he said, in a more amiable tone. "Be seeing you!"

"You're going? If I run into any snags — "

"You'll have to make out as best you can. I'm off now." The impatient note was in evidence again. "Don't go wandering around in the dark, unless you're anxious to break your neck. There are some nasty potholes after the heavy rain we've been having."

I might wrench an ankle, but I was hardly likely to break my neck by blundering into a pot-hole, I thought, puzzled by what seemed like an unnecessary warning.

"Well, thanks, but — " I began, but he had already swung on his heel. My torch beam picked out his stocky form against the white of the caravans. Then he had turned off between two of them and was lost to sight.

3

I WONDERED if 'old Westcott's' nephew had been letting caravans privately since the official closing of the camp. This particular caravan had almost certainly been recently occupied. There were unmistakable signs . . . cigarette stubs in a saucer, roughly folded blankets on one bed, a half-full kettle of water, an unwashed glass in the sink, and used tins in the waste bin under the sink.

A conscientious landlord would scarcely leave caravans in this condition during the winter, I surmised. They would be cleaned up, and the bedding and gas cylinders removed. It wasn't for me to look askance at that young man's actions, though. He had provided me with a welcome roof over my head. Admittedly, he had charged what seemed a steep price for it, but at least he hadn't objected to the puppy.

The puppy was very young. At a guess,

he couldn't be more than eight weeks old. I had begun to house-train him, but the training would obviously take a few weeks to become wholly effective. It was a miracle that he had survived. It had been touch and go.

"He's perking up," Booby had encouraged me, as I had fed him with spoonfuls of warm milk and glucose. "Yes, he is. He's really perking up . . . "

She had used that phrase repeatedly in the next day or two, and so I had named the pup 'Perkin'. He was basically a perky little fellow, but he was cold and hungry now.

I took him out on the trampled, soggy grass for a minute or so. Then I tucked him up in the blankets.

"Back soon. Stay there, Perkin." I admonished him.

I had had the forethought to pack a bottle of milk and the puppy meal and tins I had bought for him at the village stores this morning. Had it been only this morning? Yes, of course. Micky had gone off in my car, and I'd walked along to the village with the shopping party. Members of the commune had taken it in turns to acquire provisions and to provide the two main meals. I had already done my stint, but I had gone with the others to buy milk for the pup. As, head bent against the icy, stormy wind, I struggled back to the Peugeot, I thought again how the merest chance could affect main issues. If it hadn't been for Greta's protests about the puppy, and her grudging him even bread and milk, I shouldn't have been in Mrs Hickson's small, overcrowded stores this morning. I shouldn't, while responding to Mrs Hickson's professional smiles and chatter, have noticed the sleight of hand with which Lettice had been sliding tins into her shopping bag. She had been concealed from the counter by Foxy and another, burlier man, but I had been glancing idly round the packed shelves, in search of some alternative sustenance for Perkin.

Mrs Hickson had been temporarily out of tinned dog foods. I had just decided that I would go splash on some tins of steak and kidney for the little fellow when I had spotted Lettice's depredations . . .

Ought I to have spoken up then

and there? Probably, but a 'scene' in public was something from which I intuitively shrank. Also, to be honest, I was somewhat afraid to tackle Foxy and his burly pal on my own. I had imagined — in my foolish innocence — that, if I raised the question over the midday meal, I would have the support of the more dedicated members. It hadn't even crossed my mind that there could be any serious attempt to justify Lettice's thieving. I had been horrified when it had dawned on me that Lettice and Co were by no means alone in their practice of helping themselves.

I should have guessed, of course, that it hadn't been only the stray pheasant or rabbit that had been poached. It seemed doubtful if the ducks and chickens, which had frequently featured on the menu, had been paid for in cash. They hadn't been the usual deep-frozen birds. They had been brought in fully feathered. I had, on several occasions, been delegated to help pluck and draw them, because I had reluctantly admitted that I could. I hadn't queried their origins. I had supposed they had come direct from a local farmer. No doubt, they had . . .

I gave myself a mental shake. It was futile to fret over the goings on of the Down to Earthers. I was in no way responsible for them. Why couldn't I forget about them? Why this rankling soreness? Because Micky, whom I had trusted and very nearly loved, had introduced me to the commune? Because he had confidently expected me to fit in with them there?

I felt sore and humiliated. So, why make a song and dance about it? It must have happened to plenty of other girls before me . . . and at Micky's hands, too, if Booby was to be believed. I must try to hold on to my sense of proportion, and be thankful that I had escaped comparatively unscathed. Sooner or later, retribution would overtake the shoplifters. They would wax over-bold and try their game on in some bigger stores, where there were detectives or TV. How terrible I should have felt had I been with them, all unsuspecting when the arm of the law had descended on them! I might, however unwittingly, have become involved. That would have been a sorry blow to my parents . . .

I must sharpen my wits and walk more warily in future. I hadn't made an exactly propitious start by hiring accommodation here illicitly, but what else could I have done in my present circumstances. I would have a clear-cut explanation for 'old Westcott' if he were to turn up unexpectedly. I had paid my rent. Tomorrow, I must insist on a receipt for it.

I dived into the Peugeot's boot and fetched out the shopping bag and my hurriedly rolled-up bundle of sheets, towels and pillow-slip. Micky had warned me that the commune didn't supply towels or bed-linen. Most members settled for a sleeping bag, he had added, and he possessed an out-sized sleeping bag which I would be most welcome to share.

He had been smiling when he had made the suggestion, and I hadn't taken it seriously. I had enjoyed choosing a pair of pretty flowered drip-dry sheets with matching pillow-slips, in primrose yellow, and a couple of towels to match. I hadn't guessed that these purchases would excite the Down to Earthers' derision, or that I should be scolded by Greta for having bought 'man-made' fibres instead of pure cotton.

As I was about to close the boot, some small object, glittering in a corner, caught my eye. Involuntarily, I reached in for it. My fingers fastened round something cold and round. By the light of my torch, I perceived, in blank astonishment, that it was a ring . . . a gold ring set with three diamonds.

"How extraordinary!" I said aloud. "However did that get there?"

It certainly wasn't my property, and I hadn't noticed a diamond ring sparkling on the finger of any of my companions in the hen roost. It must belong to one of those girls, though. It could have become caught up in my bedding when Booby had helped me to strip my bunk. I couldn't evolve any better explanation. What a confounded nuisance! Now, I should have to pay a return visit to the commune . . . Even if, as seemed probable, this was only a 'dress' ring, of no great intrinsic value, I couldn't keep it.

Awkwardly, because my fingers were still cold, I slid the ring into my raincoat pocket and closed the boot. Back at the caravan, I was greeted with joyful squeals and tail-wags from Perkin. Mildly handicapped by his prancing around and nuzzling my ankles, I lit the Calor gas and proceeded to make up my bunk. Then I gave Perkin some bread and milk which he was prompt to devour.

If I'd had some tea-bags, I could have made tea. Yes, and if I'd had a rump steak and some potatoes, I could have partaken of grilled steak and chips! 'If onlys' weren't going to appease my hunger. My evening meal would have to consist of a chunk of bread, half a cup of milk, and a small portion of a chocolate bar, which I found in the bottom of the shopping bag.

At least, the caravan was dry and draught-proof. For the rest, I had only myself to blame. Instead of driving off into the blue in a rage, I should have made plans. I should have checked the petrol. I should have looked for a stores and bought some provisions. I should have headed for Weymouth rather than for the coast road above the Chesil Beach.

"Hope for the best. Prepare for the worst, and take what comes . . . " I couldn't remember who had said that, but it was sound advice. I chewed the brown bread and sipped the milk and tried to count my blessings.

As usual with me, the aftermath of a storm of emotion was a sense of exhaustion. My eyes began to close. I roused myself to undress. I could be thankful that I had brought pyjamas and a warm dressing-gown with me, rather than some of my more glamorous night-wear.

I was hanging up the damp rain-coat when I remembered the ring. I retrieved it and held it up to the light. Did imitation diamonds sparkle so brilliantly? But — surely not even one of those haphazard Down to Earthers would have left a genuine diamond ring lying on her bedside locker? I turned the ring this way and that with deepening uneasiness. The gold had an old and solid look about it. It felt heavy, too. Seeing it on someone's finger, I would have guessed it to be

Victorian. The design was certainly old-fashioned. My mother possessed a ring very much the same, except that hers held a ruby between two diamonds. Mrs Forrester, too, owned one similar to this, I vaguely remembered. Mrs Forrester had quite a collection of moderately valuable jewellery. She had affected to despise 'ornamentation' in any form and had openly deplored the interest her second daughter, Diana, had evinced in 'pretty things'. Sometimes, though, in one of her more human moods, Mrs Forrester had allowed the children to explore the contents of the old-fashioned, padded jewel-box which had been their grandmother's. I had a sudden, mental picture of little Diana's sliding a ring identical with this one over her thumb — and then wailing because it had stuck there. I'd had to apply soap to the ring to remove it.

Coincidence? What else could it be? There was absolutely no way in which one of Mrs Forrester's rings could have become entangled in my sheets. The sheets had still been in their cellophane wrapping when I had made up my bunk at the commune. Besides, Mrs Forrester rarely wore her jewellery and certainly did not leave stray items of it in the nursery quarters.

No, the ring must assuredly have come from the commune. I could swear that it hadn't been in the boot before today. The Peugeot was the first brand-new car I had ever bought, and I looked after her like a mother. Micky had teased me about the way in which I washed and polished her coachwork and kept the interior swept. We'd exchanged some heated remarks on one occasion, after he had borrowed her. He had brought her back with an overflowing ash-tray, ash spilt on the carpet, and the reek of stale smoke clinging to the seats. I had known that he smoked, but I hadn't supposed he ever smoked so heavily or in such a slovenly fashion.

He had called me 'fussy' and 'old-maidish'. I had retaliated by warning him that such over-indulgence in tobacco could lead to dire results.

"Not guilty! It was the fellow I gave a lift to who sullied your precious carpet by chain-smoking," Micky had defended himself.

"Then I wish you wouldn't give people lifts in my car," I had countered.

"Come now, Curly, you're not really as prim as you sound . . . "

Once again, he had disarmed and beguiled me. Perhaps it was partly due to my training and partly due to my being an only child, but I was obliged to concede that I did attach too much importance to neatness and order. Ragged sweaters, stained jeans, and laddered tights were simply not for me. I had often wondered uneasily if, despite my love for children and animals and my yearnings for a husband and a home, I had been designed for spinsterhood.

I had better tuck this tiresome ring away somewhere safely, pending inquiries about its ownership, I decided. It could be valuable. I glanced round the caravan in search of a suitable hiding-place. Why I didn't just drop it into my handbag, I couldn't have said, unless it was that, inanimate object though it was, I had conceived an intuitive distaste for it. I never had cared for the hard glitter of diamonds . . .

It must have been past midnight when I was roused from a restless sleep by the puppy's whimpers. As a children's nurse, I was easily awoken. To have to get up in the night to minister to one of my charges was nothing new. Resignedly, I fumbled for my slippers and dressing-gown. I carried the puppy down the steps to the grass, not troubling to retrieve my torch. To my surprise and relief, the skies had cleared. Moon and stars were shining, and the mist had vanished. I could see quite a long way; right down to the shimmering water. As I had guessed, this site was within a few minutes' walk of the beach. Fields sloped away from the camp to a dark mass which I guessed was an extensive reed-bed.

I fancied that Micky had brought me to that beach — or one very similar — on our way to the commune. He had said that it was a favourite haunt of bird-watchers. I must have told him that my father was keen on bird-watching, but I had wondered why Micky had supposed that rather desolate, wind-swept stretch of beach would appeal to me. I preferred a milder, more wooded scene. However, on that sunny afternoon, and before the seeds of disillusionment had begun to grow, I hadn't been disposed to fault Micky or his actions. It had been the start of our holiday and I had been determined to enjoy it.

This was certainly a peaceful spot in which to spend my second week. Perhaps I hadn't blundered too badly after all. Micky was unlikely to look for me here.

Lights . . . lights on the beach. Two lights. Anglers? Possibly. The lights were moving; heading away from the shore. After a moment or two, they were extinguished. Probably because the anglers had regained their car. No, not a car. A motor cycle. On the still air, the sound of its revving up was unmistakable.

Perkin was nudging my ankles. I picked him up and carried him back to bed, with an automatic: "Good boy! Nice, clean boy!"

As I snuggled down again, I could hear the roar of the motor cycle's engine, growing louder as it raced up the road which, I supposed, led down to the shore. Then, suddenly, the sound ceased. Uneasiness stirred in me, but I tried to squash it. I had no reason to imagine that the rider had stopped at the camp with his passenger. There must be houses not far away. Hadn't 'old Westcott's' nephew spoken of neighbours? Or, possibly, he was the rider. He might well be occupying one of the caravans, while he completed the closing-down process. If he was a dedicated angler, keen on night fishing, that was no concern of mine. He had warned me to 'keep a low profile', hadn't he? Exactly what had he meant? "Keep your nose out of my affairs"?

Excellent advice, I thought grimly. At the commune, I had been accused of being a 'busybody', a 'Nosey Parker', a 'petty sneak', and a 'spy for the cops'. In future, no matter what I chanced to witness, I would mind my own business.

4

"WHO the heck are you — and what are you doing here?"

"I was just about to put the same questions to you," I retorted.

He was standing beside my car. When, with Perkin trotting beside me, I had emerged from among the caravans, he had been peering through the windscreen. Perkin had greeted him with his funny little puppy bark and the man had turned sharply.

He was a complete stranger, tall and thin — lanky, in fact — with lean, pointed features. A navy blue woollen cap, with an absurd red tassel, hid his hair. Large, black-framed glasses made it difficult to see his eyes. He was wearing a fisherman's thick-knit sweater in natural coloured wool and baggy corduroy slacks in faded khaki.

Not an impressive figure, by any means, though his voice was pleasing, low but distinct. Incongruously enough, considering his undistinguished appearance, his voice held a note of authority.

"Have you been breaking and entering?" he demanded.

"Certainly not!" I marched up to him, chin in the air. "I've hired a caravan for a week."

"Indeed? The Camp is offically closed."

"So I understand, but the owner's nephew made an exception in my case."

"Indeed?" he repeated sceptically. "Now why would he do that?"

"He hadn't much of an alternative. I ran out of petrol last night and only just managed to coast down here," I explained.

"Out of petrol? Can't you do better than that? It's such a very old and hackneyed excuse."

"In this instance, it happens to be true. See for yourself!"

With a flourish, I held out the Peugeot's keys. To my chagrin, he took them from me and unlocked the driver's door. Then, with some difficulty, he slid his long legs in under the wheel. He switched on the ignition and peered at the gauge.

"Satisfied?" I asked tartly.

"At a guess, you've around two gallons in the tank," he answered coldly.

"What? Let me see!"

I peered in over his shoulder. Sure enough, the gauge was registering about a quarter full.

"*Oh!*" I said blankly. "He must have brought some petrol along early this morning, without rousing me."

"*He?*"

"The nephew. Mr Westcott's nephew," I said impatiently. "He was here last night, to close down the site."

"That's extremely interesting!"

"Is it? Why?" I asked blankly.

"Because, to the best of my knowledge, I happen to be Graham Westcott's one and only nephew, and I helped my uncle to close down a fortnight ago," he informed me, with a quizzical lift of his brows.

"Oh!" I felt both foolish and deflated. "He — the man who took my rent money — said he was the nephew. Can you prove that you are — and that he was an impostor?"

"Quite easily. My wallet is in my jacket pocket. If you care to step up to the office, I'll show you my banker's card and driving licence."

"As I don't know your name or his, that won't establish anything."

"No? Except that I do happen to have the keys . . . " to the office and shop and my uncle's bungalow. Uncle Graham's a careful man. It's improbable that he would give anyone a chance to steal his keys."

"All right." I knew when I was beaten. "I'll take your word for it, Mr — "

"Heston. Shadrack Heston. My mother was Winifred Westcott; Graham's sister."

"And she married a Mr Heston? How very interesting!"

"One might consider that, in your position, irony is misplaced," he said mildly. "You claim to have paid rent for a caravan, Miss — "

"Helen Melville. Yes. I paid £50."

"You have a receipt, of course?"

"No. I haven't. It was wet and dark and all I wanted was to get under cover. He said he'd bring me the receipt when he brought the petrol."

"An odd story. It could be true, of course . . . "

"It is true! Why on earth shouldn't it be? Do I look like the kind of person who would break into a caravan?" I flashed.

"No, you don't. You don't look, either, as if you were wanted by the police."

"Wanted? By the police?" I gaped at him. "Is this a joke?"

"I wouldn't know. Is it? Have you been creating a public nuisance? Demonstrating or writing on walls?"

"Certainly not. I'm not at all that kind of person. I'm not a student, anyway. I'm a qualified children's nurse," I said, with what dignity I could muster. "The police have nothing on me."

"Then, why are they searching for this car?"

"This car? My car?" I gasped. "They can't be."

"I heard it on the radio. A yellow Peugeot, registration BTT 9990. 'Will the driver or any persons who can give information as to the car's whereabouts, please get in touch with the nearest police station or ring Plymouth . . . ' I've forgotten the number," he quoted. "Must be this car."

"Plymouth? I haven't been near

Plymouth for over a week. I was at Malbury, a few miles out of Plymouth, but I left last Saturday morning."

"Is that so? How very interesting!"

It wasn't quite sarcasm, but my skin burned.

"Sorry!" I said impulsively. "I'm not really such a crabby character, but you contrived to put me in the wrong."

"A rare achievement, I should imagine."

"If that's a compliment, thanks . . . but I've made a proper mess of my holiday this year. Can you imagine anything more feckless than to strand oneself on a stormy Saturday night in October, with no petrol and no provisions?"

"Could have been worse. Could have been January," he offered, and for the first time a smile lit up his bony features. No provisions? That's tough! You must be starving."

"I am."

"Then, suppose you come up to the bungalow with me and we'll rustle up some breakfast. I've been out since dawn and I'm hungry, too."

"Since dawn? What have you been doing? Bird watching?"

"Precisely. Trying for photographs . . . "

He produced one of those tiny but highly efficient and professional cameras from the pocket of his slacks.

"Lovely job, isn't it? My father's saving up for one," I said involuntarily. "Not that he's much of a photographer, but he's dead keen . . . "

His smile deepened, and I added defensively: "That's very interesting! I'll say it for you."

"No need for the hedgehog act, Helen. Mind if I call you 'Helen'? It's a favourite name of mine, and, if we're to be fellow sojourners here for the remainder of the week, it would seem unnecessarily formal to stick to Mr and Miss."

I hesitated. In other circumstances, I might have retorted that I was a formal kind of person. In these circumstances, such an assertion would have appeared ludicrous. He would, inevitably, classify it as part of my 'hedgehog act'. I had been called 'stand-offish' and 'snobby', but nobody before had called me a 'hedgehog'.

"I've certainly no desire to typify a hedgehog," I said stiffly.

"Offended? Apart from their prickles, hedgehogs are rather endearing creatures."

"They may seem so, and undoubtedly they're a boon to gardeners, but they're usually covered in fleas," I said distastefully.

At that, he burst out laughing. He had a pleasant, oddly youthful laugh, which was infectious enough to make me join in it reluctantly.

"We seem fated to rub up each other's fur the wrong way, don't we? I wasn't for a moment implying that you weren't fastidious in your grooming," he grinned. "Come on, now! Let's call a truce. My name's Shadrack . . . "

"As in the Bible? Shadrack, Meshech and Abednego," I asked curiously.

"Exactly. You're obviously well-read," he said approvingly. "'Shadrack' foxes a great many people."

"I'm a parson's daughter," I explained. "It's an uncommon name. Any specific reason for your being called by it?"

"Yes." His smile vanished. His bony features took on a withdrawn look. "That's a nice pup you have there — " as Perkin tentatively nosed his ankles.

"What d'you call him?"

"Perkin."

"After Perkin Warbeck?"

"Oh, no!"

Almost without my realising it, we had turned away from the car and were walking sedately up the concrete drive down which I had coasted last night. So — what? It would be senseless to turn down the offer of a hot meal, simply because Shadrack Heston had the same effect on my skin as a cluster of burdock burrs penetrating my tights.

What if he was an irritating and tactless character? Hadn't I had my fill of suave charm? Besides, if he was 'old Westcott's one and only nephew', I was at his mercy; at least, financially. He hadn't received my £50. He could, I supposed, send me packing, if he chose.

As we walked, with Perkin skipping around our ankles, I explained briefly what had led to my landing myself with the puppy.

"A heroic rescue. Helen's a heroic and romantic name," Shadrack commented. "Do you consciously live up to it?"

"Of course not. I don't like heroics.

Anyway, that pond was merely smelly and unpleasant. I don't suppose it was more than four feet deep, even in the middle," I said hastily. "Come to that, Shadrack is much more symbolic of heroism. The Bible Shadrack was a fantastically brave young man."

He nodded and quickened his stride, so that I had some difficulty in keeping up with him. Near the top of the drive, there was a small iron gate, which I hadn't noticed in the darkness last night. Shadrack opened the gate for me, and closed it after us. I stepped on to a narrow path between banks of flowering shrubs. The path emerged on to a smooth expanse of lawn, a small paved terrace, and a bungalow with pink-washed walls and a lime-green tiled roof.

"Nice!" I said appreciatively. "Your uncle's?"

"During the season, while he's running the camp, he lives here. Out of season, I rent it for a nominal sum, and spend most weekends here."

"Bird watching?" I said brightly.

"Mainly, yes." He fished in his pockets and brought out a bunch of keys. As he fitted the appropriate key into the lock of the neat white door, he said: "The Sunday papers should be here soon. They should provide a clue."

"A clue? To what?"

He turned to look at me sharply and appraisingly.

"A reason why the police should be searching for you and your car," he said — as if to a singularly dense child. "Aren't you even curious about their burning desire to interview you?"

"There isn't any. I mean, it's nonsense. Somebody must have made a mistake in the registration number," I said flatly. "The police can't possibly have any reason for wanting to interrogate *me*. I haven't been concerned in an accident. You need only to examine my car to see that she hasn't a scratch on her."

"You could have run somebody down without damaging your car."

"Improbable. Anyway, I haven't run anybody down. I would know it if I had, wouldn't I?" I said impatiently. "It's far more likely that you confused the number of the wanted car with the emergency call. I mean, everybody knows to dial 999 for an ambulance or a fire engine or the police. I was given a choice of registration numbers, and I chose one I couldn't forget. My last car was 276, and I kept on getting it muddled, because my telephone number at home is 267."

"Feminine logic!" he said, with an irritating assumption of masculine superiority. "Not very convincing, Helen."

"Sorry about that — Shadrack."

"No papers yet," he pronounced, turning to survey the empty letterbox. "Let's wait till they arrive before we resume hostilities. Until we are in possession of the facts, speculation is pointless. So are your defensive tactics."

"I'm not — " I began. Then I checked myself. "Sorry! I do sound edgy."

"You're hungry," he conceded, and led me along a short passage into a small but adequately equipped kitchen. "Smoked mackerel, grilled, with toast and coffee?"

"Sounds marvellous."

I might have surmised that he wouldn't go for the conventional bacon and eggs. In spite of his somewhat nondescript appearance, he wasn't, I decided, at all a nondescript character.

"You can make the toast," he said — as if he wouldn't trust me not to burn the mackerel. "There's the toaster and there's a sliced loaf in the bread-bin."

He fetched the fillets of mackerel from the refrigerator. I watched absorbedly as with swift, economical movements he transferred the fillets to the grill, sprinkled them with black pepper, and dabbed them with liberal pats of dairy butter.

"You're a cook?" I hazarded. "Fond of cooking?"

"Used to cooking for myself," he amended.

"Do you fish?"

"Occasionally."

"If you were out at dawn, presumably you weren't out fishing from the shore till midnight?"

"Last night? No. Why do you ask?"

"Because somebody was. At least, I saw lights on the beach. I wondered who could be keen enough to stand out there on such a rough night. It was calmer at midnight, of course, but still chilly."

"Were you wandering around at midnight? Not very sensible."

"I wasn't. I merely had to let Perkin out . . . and I noticed the lights." I turned from the bread-bin, my brows puckering. "Do odd things happen around here at night?"

"Sometimes, I believe. What gives you reason to suppose so?"

"That man — the one who took my £50 — warned me to stay put and keep a low profile. You've just hinted that I shouldn't wander around after dark."

"I was speaking generally. He warned you, did he? That's — "

"Very interesting," I finished for him.

"I was going to say 'significant'. Obviously, the fellow was up to no good here. Describe him!"

"Not so easy. He was all muffled up . . . hooded and anoraked. Stocky in build, and, I think, swarthy, but I caught only a glimpse of his face by torchlight."

"Anoraks tend to make people look bulky."

Nothing could make Shadrack look bulky, I thought amusedly. He was a regular bean-pole. He had pulled off the knitted cap and hung it on a hook in the passage, revealing a thatch, short cut, of exceedingly ordinary mouse-brown hair. Apart from his height and boniness, he was ordinary looking. He wasn't even what was commonly called 'attractively ugly'. Compared with Micky, Shadrack was downright plain. Yet, somehow, there was this odd distinctiveness about him.

I hadn't, even when I had been almost sure I would marry Micky, looked forward to taking him home and presenting him to my parents. I had foreseen that, in spite of his charm and tact, he would fail to endear himself to them.

Shadrack had no such obvious assets, yet I knew already that I could take him home without a qualm. He would be entirely at his ease with my parents and they with him.

What an absurd train of thought! I had only just met this man — and so far we had persistently clashed. Yes, but openly and without malice, I reasoned. I, who must have seemed dumb and withdrawn, or purposefully aloof, among Micky's friends in the commune, could talk freely to Shadrack Heston. He was my kind of person. We spoke the same tongue. Possibly we had sprung from the same kind of background. 'Like to like'? Or the much vaunted 'attraction of opposites'? Which was the more compulsive? Both could exert a strong magnetism.

"Lost in thought, Helen?" Shadrack inquired. "The toast rack is in the cupboard above the toaster."

"What? Oh, sorry!"

I became belatedly aware that the toaster had performed its given function and that two nicely browned slices of toast had popped up from it. I opened the cupboard and got out the toast-rack. I fed the toaster with two more slices of bread.

"Worried?" he asked sympathetically. "No need to be, if you've a cast-iron alibi."

"Alibi? Why should I need an alibi?"

"If a car like yours has been involved in a serious accident, you may be glad of an alibi."

"Possibly."

Surely, Micky would have told me if

he had run into any trouble yesterday morning? Where had he gone in the Peugeot? I hadn't a clue. I didn't even know when he had started. I had, at his request, handed over the keys on Friday night.

"If it's a fine morning, I may make an early start," he had informed me. "No need to wake you."

"I wouldn't mind. I could go with you," I had suggested, but he had shaken his head emphatically.

"Too boring for you, my love, to hang around, nibbling your finger nails, while I discuss business terms with my clients," he had said glibly. "It would cramp my style to know that you were waiting. You'll have more fun here."

'Fun'? Did he really imagine that I was having any 'fun' among the Down to Earthers? He should have shown more perception, I had thought at the time, with heightened qualms. Really, the man didn't know me at all. Had he done the whole of the talking on our dates in Plymouth? Or hadn't he listened to anything I had said? I was certain I had told him that I would rather give than lend a cherished possession. It must have registered on him that I was exceedingly loth to lend my car . . .

Perhaps that was why, if he'd had an accident, he hadn't owned up about it. Not that he'd had much of a chance, I recalled. As soon as he had rejoined us, I had raised the matter of the stolen tins. After that furore, except for those scant minutes in the hen roost, before Booby had barged in on us, he'd had no opportunity of getting me on my own.

A delicious aroma was proceeding from the sizzling mackerel. I realised that I was ravenously hungry. I removed the second batch of toast and fed in a third.

"It's grand to meet a girl who's not afraid to eat," Shadrack said approvingly, ten minutes later. "Most disheartening to prepare tasty dishes for females who barely nibble at them."

"Do you often? Entertain diet-conscious females?" I asked impulsively.

"On and off. When my lone, lorn bachelor existence begins to pall. No special girl at the moment," he answered frankly. "What about yourself?"

"I haven't had any facilities for

entertaining friends — male or female. I've been living in other people's houses, looking after their children for them," I explained. "I worked for 'Kiddy Care', doing temporary jobs."

"Worked?"

"I'm not sure if I'll be given another assignment or not. My last one ended disastrously."

"How was that?"

"I lost my temper with one of my charges and spanked her," I admitted wryly. "Dead against the 'Kiddy Care' rules."

He glanced up from his toast and marmalade to give me a long, appraising look from behind his glasses. I couldn't be sure of the expression in his eyes, but his lips were quirking upwards amusedly.

"You wouldn't appear to have a violent temper. No doubt, the child deserved the spanking," he pronounced.

"I certainly thought so, but the fact remains that I broke the rules."

It was surprisingly easy to talk to him. I found myself telling him all about Mrs Forrester and her family.

"She's not an animal person. She

didn't care a scrap about that beautiful pony. It's simply a prestige thing. To have a child who shines at gymkhanas, I mean," I finished indignantly. "Caroline was just the same. She adored winning rosettes and cups, but she expected me to groom and feed the pony."

"A spoilt brat?"

"I thought so. And not affectionate or endearing, as some over-indulged children can be."

"So . . . you're on holiday now?"

"Yes."

Somehow, I was loth to tell him about Micky and the commune.

I asked instead: "What do you do? Help to run this camp?"

"Oh, heavens, no! I wouldn't have the tact or the patience. I'm an accountant. I audit Uncle's accounts for him and deal with his Income Tax and VAT returns. He's marvellous with his guests. He's one of those big, hearty, genial men who genuinely like people and can make any party go. Hopeless with figures, though."

There was a slight thud from the passage. Perkin, who had been curled into a fluffy ball at my feet, fast asleep, sat up and gave his funny little puppy bark.

"The Sunday papers. Help yourself to some more coffee," Shadrack said hospitably, uncoiling himself from his chair and heading for the door. "I'll get the papers. There may be something in them to solve the mystery of that broadcast appeal."

"You still won't take my word for it that I'm not involved?"

I couldn't keep a hurt note out of my voice. We had been getting on swimmingly together, or so I had thought, but it seemed that he still mistrusted me.

"I don't like unsolved mysteries. As an accountant, I've been trained to investigate . . . "

"To probe and pry into people's private affairs?" I flashed.

"If you care to put it that way, yes. To attempt to conceal facts and figures from your accountant can be highly dangerous," he retorted coolly.

"You're not my accountant — and I don't have anything to conceal."

"Lucky you!"

With that he vanished into the passage. Nobody could get the better of Shadrack in an argument, I decided angrily. He was a most exasperating person. The most exasperating thing about him was that what he said made sense.

5

"TAKE your choice," Shadrack invited me.

He put two newspapers down on the table. One was of the more intellectual type, complete with coloured supplement. The second was the 'Sunday Spotlight', a popular picture paper. Did he take the picture paper for the benefit of any female he might be entertaining for the weekend? I wondered — and deliberately reached for the bulky paper.

"I like reading the book reviews," I said. "There's never anything worth reading in that rag."

"Many thanks! I write Nature Notes for the said rag," he informed me.

"Oh, you! What a genius you have for putting people in the wrong," I snapped. "Why didn't you become a policeman or a lawyer?"

"Possibly because my father was forced into bankruptcy — and needn't have been, if he'd had a conscientious and competent accountant, instead of an incompetent fool," he answered equably, but with an undercurrent of feeling. "Father took it hard. In fact, he never recovered from what he considered the disgrace of being unable to meet all his obligations."

Once again, he had contrived to make me feel small.

"Sorry," I said awkwardly. "I don't really know the first thing about accountants or what they do."

He nodded and sat down again. He opened the 'Sunday Spotlight'. In silence, we sipped coffee and browsed through the papers.

Then, Shadrack exclaimed abruptly: "Forrester? Wasn't that your ex-employer? Millicent Forrester? High Rise, Malbury, near Plymouth?"

"Yes. That was the woman. What about her?"

"She has been robbed, apparently. Quote — 'This was certainly the most costly rosette my daughter, Caroline, has ever won', lamented attractive Millicent Forrester (36), when I interviewed her in her luxury home near Plymouth. She pointed wryly to the glass case, full of rosettes and silver trophies won by her pretty and talented little daughter. 'The thieves must have watched us leave for the Pony Club trials, and they must have had a duplicate key, because there's no sign of forcible entry' . . . "

"No! Oh, no!" I cried out incredulously. "How extraordinary!"

"That's not all. Asked if she had any suspicions about the identity of the thieves, Mrs Forrester hesitated and then spoke evasively of a former children's nurse, who had been issued with a latchkey. It was just possible, she supposed, that the key could have been 'borrowed' and a duplicate made, while it had been in the nursemaid's possession. 'She was a very pretty girl, with a host of boy friends', Mrs Forrester admitted, when pressed for details."

"Heavens!" I said, aghast. "She suspects *me*?"

"So it would appear."

"It's fantastic! I certainly never lent my latch-key."

"It could have been borrowed without your knowledge by one of that host of boy-friends," Shadrack suggested.

I felt my cheeks flaming.

"There wasn't any host. I had a few dates, yes. They didn't come to anything."

"No serious involvement?" he pressed me.

How was I to answer that? Evasiveness would convey the impression that I had something to hide. Had I? Was there any good reason to try to keep Micky out of this? Not if he were guilty in any way . . . but was he? Could he have filched my key from my handbag and put it back again before I had realised that it was missing?

"You've hesitated just too long," Shadrack said drily. "Better tell me."

"Why should I? It's no concern of yours."

"Isn't it? When you have taken refuge on my uncle's property? Do you want me to call the police and tell them your car's here?"

"I don't see what my car can have to do with it," I said rebelliously. "And I certainly wasn't near Malbury yesterday. I could easily prove that I wasn't."

"Good! There's such a thing as being an accessory, though; before or after a crime has been committed."

"Well, I'm not it — and I can't believe that Micky — "

I stopped short. The horrid memory of that glittering ring had suddenly risen up to confound me. Was it one of Millicent Forrester's? Could it be?

"*Micky?*" Shadrack took me up sharply. "Who's Micky?"

"A man I met in Plymouth. I suppose you could say that he had picked me up, but in actual fact we met at a Church 'do', a Harvest Supper. I went there with Samantha, the daughter of Mrs Forrester's daily woman, and she introduced me to Micky."

"Yes? And was it love at first sight?" he asked cynically.

"Of course not."

"Then — "

"He laid himself out to be agreeable. He had a great deal of charm," I said slowly. "A friend of Samantha's joined us, and he seemed quite pleasant, too. When Micky suggested a foursome — to the cinema — and there was a film

85

I particularly wanted to see — there seemed no reason to refuse."

"Yes?"

"We had two or three Saturday afternoon dates like that — as a foursome. Only I couldn't always get away on a Saturday, because I often had to take Caroline to a Pony Club 'do' or a gymkhana. So . . . gradually . . . it was Micky and I who met of an evening during the week. I was usually free after I had seen the three children to bed."

"Romance blossomed?"

"I suppose I thought so," I admitted reluctantly. "He seemed to be serious about me . . . and he is attractive. We had some quite delightful outings together. No cheap snack-bars or 'pull-ins' for Micky, and always the best seats at any show."

"What's his job?"

"He called himself an agent. He said he put buyers and sellers in touch with one another. Sometimes, he was very lavish with his money," I recalled. "Oh, it doesn't make sense! Why would he steal Mrs Forrester's jewellery? And — how could he? He wasn't anywhere near Malbury yesterday."

"Can you be sure of that? You didn't lend him your car?"

"As a matter of fact, I did, but we were staying in a village near Weymouth, a hundred miles or more from Malbury." I noted his quirked eyebrows . . . brows several shades darker than his mousy brown hair — and seethed inwardly. "No, we weren't living together, if that's what you're imagining. We were staying in a community centre, run by friends of Micky's."

"If he borrowed your car, where did he go?"

"I've no idea. I didn't ask. I can't believe that he can have rushed off to Malbury . . . "

"Can't? Or — won't?"

I made an impatient gesture.

"Do you have to interrogate me — as if you were Counsel for the Prosecution?"

"Sorry — " but he didn't sound penitent. "I was trying to prepare you for the kind of questions the police will put to you."

"The police?" I echoed in dismay.

"You'll have to get in touch with them."

"I don't have to — and I shan't," I objected. "There's absolutely nothing I can tell them . . . "

"Nothing?" Again, his brows quirked upwards sceptically.

"Nothing useful," I said obstinately.

"It would seem obvious that your car was spotted in Malbury. Yellow Peugeots aren't all that common."

I was silent. Confused and conflicting thoughts were racing round and round in my brain. If Micky was guilty of theft, had I any right to shield him? Did I even want to shield him? Perhaps not, but could I be the one to give him away?

I had cared for him. Not very deeply, I supposed, and not for very long, but we had shared some good times together. He had given me hope; the hope that one day my dreams might be fulfilled; that I might find a loving and loyal husband without having to submit myself to a number of experimental affairs first.

In the words of Samantha, the daily woman's daughter who had introduced me to Micky: "You can't help going for that fellow. He treats you right."

"You're still keen on that young man," Shadrack said severely — and as if he were many years older. "You know he's involved, but you're determined not to admit it."

"I don't *know* anything," I said, with emphasis on the verb, "and I dislike jumping to conclusions. One can be grossly unfair that way."

"Can one?"

"Undoubtedly. Didn't you jump to the conclusion that I was a fugitive from a sordid little affaire which had gone sour on me?"

He had the grace to look abashed.

"Something of the sort," he conceded. "Ravishingly lovely girls — genuine Helens — don't normally go on holiday alone."

"You see? And when I mentioned the commune, you instantly pictured a disorderly gathering with sex orgies and pot. You surmised that I'd fled from it, because I didn't enjoy that type of self-indulgence."

He pulled a wry face and inquired

mildly: "Didn't you?"

"Didn't I — what? If it's of any interest to you, I stuck it out for a week, and then felt I'd had it, but not for the reasons you surmised."

"Not?"

"No. It was disorderly only in the sense of 'untidy'. The sex was quite discreet, and there weren't any orgies. I didn't notice any signs of drug taking. The husband and wife who run the place are serious craftsmen."

I wasn't sure why I felt impelled to defend the Down to Earthers, unless it was out of a sense of loyalty to Micky. He wouldn't, I realised belatedly, have taken me to the kind of place Shadrack had seemed to be visualising. Micky had, in his own fashion, 'treated me right'.

"We're getting side-tracked," Shadrack pointed out. "This man — Micky, is it? — borrowed your car. You've admitted that."

"It's all I have admitted," I reminded him. "I simply can't believe that he robbed Mrs Forrester."

"What you really mean is that you can't bring yourself to believe that he picked you up to use as an unconscious accessory. That would have hurt your pride," Shadrack observed dispassionately.

"Certainly I can't believe it — pride or no pride. It wouldn't have been worth it, from his point of view," I countered. "He devoted hours and hours to me — and spent quite freely on our outings, too."

"The good lady's jewellery was insured for £90,000, according to the report . . ."

"If she had all that much, I never saw it," I said incredulously. "She professed to despise 'trappings'. She occasionally wore a diamond or a sapphire ring and ear-rings. Nothing elaborate."

Again there was silence between us; an awkward, antagonistic silence. My heart was thudding and there was a bitter taste in my throat. I tried to think what I ought to do. Obviously, Shadrack wouldn't care for me to stay here.

It would be ignominious to have to crawl back to the commune, and doubtful if that would provide me with a refuge. Somebody was certain to have read the Sunday Spotlight. The girls might hesitate to contact the police lest Micky should be suspected, but their menfolk wouldn't be eager to protect him — and the girls, except perhaps for Booby, would be glad to see me hauled off to the police station for interrogations.

I could almost hear Lettice saying spitefully: "That'll take her down a peg or two. Preaching at us! We don't steal jewellery . . . "

I could be thankful that my parents were in the Holy Land. They would have had a nasty shock had some officious parishioner drawn their attention to the newspaper account and Mrs Forrester's hints. At the same time, their absence meant that I couldn't go home. I had friends, of course, in the parish who would willingly have given me house-room, but I wouldn't want to involve any of them . . .

Whatever I did or didn't do, the police would almost certainly catch up with me before long. I was prepared for that. The longer I could elude their questioning, though, the better.

"Stubborn, aren't you? Blind — or at least misguided — loyalty?" Shadrack commented at last, his brows contracting.

Those dark brown eyebrows were

his most expressive feature, I thought inconsequently.

"Possibly," I answered guardedly. "Or possibly a sense of fair play. How can I condemn a man as a thief without first giving him a chance to clear himself?"

"The evidence — "

"Is all circumstantial. So far, at any rate. Does any eyewitness testify to having seen Micky at or near High Rise yesterday?"

"The police would be unlikely to mention it to the press, if they did have any such evidence."

"Someone must have reported the presence of a yellow Peugeot. Who? Does the paper say?"

"Not as far as I can see." He shrugged his bony shoulders. "Thefts are all too common these days to be given much space in the newspapers. It must have been the gymkhana — pony-angle which made some enterprising reporter look up Mrs Forrester."

"Mrs Forrester hasn't forgiven me for 'humiliating' her darling little Caroline, as she put it," I said slowly. "That's why she's ready to suspect me."

He nodded, and reached for the percolator. Only a few drops remained in it. He shrugged his shoulders again. Then he rose and began to carry our used cups and plates to the sink. From force of habit? Or because he wanted to eliminate all trace of my visit to his quarters?

"I'll do that," I offered, jumping up so hurriedly that I inadvertently trod on the sleeping puppy's thread of a tail. He squealed piteously, and I bent to soothe him.

"Sorry, pet! Sorry, Perkin. I didn't mean to hurt you," I assured him remorsefully.

Shadrack had turned from the sink at the puppy's cry. When I straightened myself he was staring at me with a wry quirk to those expressive brows.

"I don't suppose Helen of Troy meant to hurt anyone," he said quizzically. "She simply gave way to her impulses."

"If that's a hit at me, you're off-target. I'm not an impulsive person."

His brows rose higher and I gave a sigh of exasperation.

"I'd better go, hadn't I? Just give me time to get my things together from the

94

caravan . . . or do you intend to contact the police immediately?"

"No," he said shortly. "I think you're stubborn and foolish and headstrong, but not a conscious accessory. If you're determined not to talk to them, there's no point in bringing the police here."

"Well, thanks! I'll go and pack."

"No need. You'll be as safe here as anywhere, once your car's under cover. We can run the car into Uncle's private garage."

"Oh!" I drew a long deep breath. "That's very good of you, Shadrack, but aren't you making yourself an accessory? I mean, isn't that what the police will think if they catch up with me?"

"I'll have to take my chance with that. Can any man be seriously blamed for helping a lovely lady in distress?" He grinned unexpectedly. "I can plead that you bewitched me."

"Nobody would swallow that."

"No? It's not all that far from the truth."

He was trying to make me rise. He could scarcely be serious. Most men would call me 'pretty'. Micky

95

had, on occasion, told me that I was 'lovely'. Nobody would consider me an enchantress. For enchantment, one needed beautiful, seductive clothes, fine jewels, an alluring perfume, and an attractive background.

"Why are you smiling?" Shadrack inquired.

I told him and he laughed.

"Don't be so conventional, Helen! Enchantment can come in all shapes and sizes."

"Not in a sweater, trouser suit, and gumboots," I said firmly.

"Practical, and a sense of humour, too," he said approvingly. "You've a lot going for you."

"Thanks."

I was conscious of a deep sense of relief. The strain and tension between us had vanished, swept away by laughter. Perkin seemed conscious of it, too. He pranced around us, tail curled gaily over his back, as we headed for the door. Already, the pup was swift to sense my moods.

Once again, there was a feeling of companionship between Shadrack and me, as if we were old and tried friends. Somehow, he would hit on a solution to these disturbing mysteries, I thought confidently; a solution which would absolve both me and Micky of any complicity in the robbery.

We turned out of the shrubbery path into the concrete drive — to be brought up short. My growing sense of well-being was abruptly shattered. My yellow Peugeot had disappeared. I stared unbelievingly at the empty drive . . .

6

"MY car has gone . . . " I said stupidly. "She's not there, where I left her. Someone must have taken her."

"Obviously."

"But — when? And who? I didn't hear anything . . . "

"With cars passing up and down the road fairly frequently, it's unlikely that we should have noticed when yours was driven up the drive." His dark brown brows contracted. "Blast! I should have thought earlier about concealing the car. We shouldn't have left her here, in the open."

"We hadn't seen that news item in the paper when we left her," I reminded him. "Could the police have spotted her and towed her away?"

"The police would have called at the bungalow and made inquiries about the car's owner."

"Then — who?"

"Most probably, that fellow who rooked you of £50. It looks as if he's in residence here, somewhere," Shadrack said grimly. "Or was. He may have seen me arrive and decided to beat it."

"In my car?"

"On the other hand, he may simply have borrowed your car. He may be unaware that the police are on the look-out for her. In that case, he may be in for a nasty shock."

"That won't help *me*. If the car is stopped by the police and they impound her, what do I do?"

"That's up to you. If you were to report the theft of your car . . . "

"To the police? Oh, no! They would insist on my telling them where the car was yesterday morning. That is, if it was seen in Malbury."

"Isn't there someone in Malbury whom you could contact? Someone who could give you more details of the Forrester robbery?" Shadrack suggested. "You had other friends, apart from this Micky?"

"I wasn't there long enough to get to know many people . . . and I don't make friends easily," I had to admit. "There's

Samantha, of course. She more or less took me up for a while; until Micky and I began to pair off together."

"Why not get in touch with her?"

"How? She lives with her widowed mother and they haven't a telephone."

"Where does she work?"

"As a hotel receptionist . . . but this is Sunday."

"Doesn't she ever work on Sundays?" he persisted.

"Sometimes," I said reluctantly.

Why was he so eager for further details? Couldn't he take my word for it that I wasn't in any way involved?

"You could try."

He was shepherding me back towards the bungalow. I couldn't think of any good reason why I should turn down what was basically a sensible suggestion, yet it was with a curious feeling of foreboding that I dialled the Malbury number of the White Frog. I found myself hoping fervently that Samantha wouldn't be on duty, but it was her unmistakable high-pitched and somewhat affected voice which answered my call.

"Samantha? This is Helen," I said

tentatively. "I've just heard the news. Read it, I mean."

"Just heard it? That's rich! Playing it cool, are we?"

"I don't know what you mean. Tell me — "

"What can I tell you?" Again she didn't give me time to finish the sentence. "I bet you're furious with me, aren't you? I didn't want to give you away, but they simply forced it out of me. They came round to our flat last night and poor Mum got fearfully upset. She was scared that they were suspecting her."

"They? The police, do you mean?"

"Who else? So I had to tell them. Honestly, I had no choice. Anyway, other people must have noticed it, too. Why on earth didn't you borrow something less eye-catching?"

"What are you talking about? My car?"

"Of course. You shouldn't have left it so near what they call 'the scene of the crime'. Lots of passers-by must have noticed it. You were on the double lines, too. A Traffic Warden might easily have run you in for illegal parking." She gave a high-pitched giggle. "*Really*, Helen, it was all terribly amateurish. Why did you do it? Just to get your own back on that Forrester woman?"

"I didn't. I wasn't anywhere near Malbury yesterday," I said desperately. "It can't have been my car you saw."

"BTT 9990? That's your number, isn't it? I remember it because of Syd's silly joke. 'You could have bought a Mini cheaper, but you had to go one better than the crowd'. Wasn't that what he said? He thought you were fearfully snooty. He'll have a good laugh now when the cops catch up with you."

"Samantha, listen! You've got it all wrong . . . "

"Who says?" She giggled again. "Sorry, ducks! I'll have to ring off now. There's quite a queue at the desk, waiting for the Sunday papers . . . "

The 'phone went dead. I turned slowly. Shadrack was standing beside me. One glance at his expressive brows warned me that Samantha's high-pitched soprano had reached him quite clearly.

"She's lying," I said flatly. "She must be."

"She could have seen your car," he said dispassionately. "You can't prove that she wasn't in Malbury."

"Parked on double yellow lines? Oh, no! Micky may be many things I don't know about, but I'm sure he isn't a fool. If he were planning a robbery, he certainly wouldn't risk inciting the attention of a Traffic Warden."

"Possibly he hadn't any option."

"It would have been safer to have parked the car in the Forresters' drive, where it would have been screened from the road by a belt of firs," I retorted. "High Rise is in a short residential road, not much more than a lane. The main road into Plymouth runs at the bottom of the lane. That's where the double yellow lines are. Micky would never have parked there."

I hadn't convinced him. I could deduce that from the sceptical tilt of his expressive brows, and the tightened line of his lips.

"Why would the girl — a friend of yours — fabricate such a story?" he demanded.

"Search me!" I was baffled and

somewhat hurt. I had thought of Samantha Tiggs as a friend. When I had first arrived at High Rise, Samantha had sought me out and made much of me. "You heard her. She didn't sound particularly friendly."

"No. More as if she were gloating over your predicament," Shadrack conceded. "A kind of 'How are the mighty fallen!' scoffing."

I flinched.

"I expect that's how the Down to Earthers will react — if and when they get around to connecting me with the robbery," I said wryly. "Most of them thought me absurdly prim and prudish. Perhaps Samantha did, too, secretly, although she pretended to share my views."

"Going one better?" he quoted. "Who's Syd?"

"You must have remarkably acute hearing."

"I have, and your friend has a remarkably penetrating voice. Syd?" he repeated.

"Sydney Tane. Samantha's current boy-friend. To their particular gang,

104

they were known as Tiggs and Tane," I answered, with a reminiscent frown. "Syd tended to hang round Micky and sometimes ran errands for him. A bit of a creep, I thought him. Squirmy and ingratiating and for ever making feeble jokes."

"You would appear to have chosen some odd companions," Shadrack commented drily.

"Oh, it's easy to criticise or to be wise after the event! You try being all alone in the suburb of a big city. It's not so hot, believe me!" I said feelingly. "I'm not a good mixer. I couldn't barge into a popular café or disco and instantly find suitable friends. When I had time off, how could I spend it? Window shopping? Changing my library books? Sitting in my bedroom, reading or needleworking? Going for solitary walks? At the cinema? I did all those things."

"I'm often in a strange town, when I'm on a job . . . but I guess it's different for a girl. Tougher," he said reflectively. "Unless you've any absorbing hobby and can join a Club . . . "

"As I was rarely on an assignment for

longer than a month, it didn't seem worth while to join anything," I said regretfully. "I was grateful to Mrs Tiggs for inviting me to her flat, and grateful to Samantha for welcoming me."

"What sort of girl is she?"

"Lively and sparkling. Attractive in a gipsyish fashion. Go-ahead, and reputedly witty. Quick with wise-cracks and repartee. Good company. The boys flocked round her," I said unenviously. "She could take her pick."

"She could have picked Micky?"

That was an unexpected and shrewd question. I looked at him with respect.

"You think Samantha might have resented it, when Micky picked me?"

"Didn't she?"

"I don't know," I answered frankly. "She didn't show it. She seemed happy enough with Sydney, when the four of us went out together."

"Later?"

"I didn't see much of her. Micky monopolised my free time."

"It all comes back to this Micky. You can't go on shielding him, Helen. You know very well that he's guilty,"

Shadrack said severely. "You've made yourself an accessory, by letting him borrow your key and your car."

"I did not lend him my key."

I could see that he didn't believe me. Samantha had sounded too convincing. Why, on the face of it, should she lie? She must have seen my car in Malbury . . .

"Helen, I wish you would be frank with me . . ."

Shadrack moved towards me, and put his hands firmly on my arms. His touch sent a curious tremor through me. I wanted to wrench myself free, and yet I didn't. There was something comforting about his clasp. It took away that unnerving feeling of being utterly alone in a tight spot.

"You don't believe me. You don't trust me," I said unsteadily.

"You're not trusting *me*."

"Why should I trust *you*?"

We looked at each other challengingly; two strangers, who had met by the merest chance; if indeed anything happened by mere chance. My mother would reason that we ourselves by our own thoughts and actions were responsible directly or indirectly for the events which involved us. My father would say that the Almighty had a pattern for everyone's life and that 'all things work together for good'.

"Why? Because you're you and I'm I. Because . . . " His hands tightened on my arms. "How can I put it without sounding cheap or trite? You know."

Yes. I knew. I knew there was some kind of recognition between us; some kind of flicker. Anything might happen as a result. We might stamp out or douche the first tentative sparks. We might fan them into a warm and lasting fire. It was all too tentative to be put into words.

"Yes," I said slowly. "I do trust you. At least, I think I do. Only — "

"Only, there's this Micky. If you're not in love with him — "

He paused inquiringly.

"In love?" I echoed. "The phrase slips so easily off the tongue, doesn't it? But — what does it mean? Who's to say? Who's to know? How strongly does one have to care for a person to be certain one is 'in love'?"

"You're right," he said, after a brief pause. "It's much too glib. It's used too often and too lightly. Let me word it differently. How far are you prepared to go to protect this man?"

"That's even more difficult to answer," I groaned. "I'm not sure that I do want to 'protect' him. It's more that I owe him something and I'm determined to be fair to him."

"More than fair."

He sounded disgruntled; like the jealous husband of tradition, but that was plainly absurd. Why in the world should he be jealous over me; a complete stranger? I might equally well be jealous of all the girls he had entertained here.

He must have sensed my inward withdrawal. He released his hold of me abruptly.

"You can borrow my car," he jerked out, as if with reluctance.

"Borrow your car? Why?"

"You'll have to see him; question him."

He was right, I realised. I would have to face Micky again. I would have to give him a chance to prove that he hadn't been in Malbury yesterday. Distasteful though the prospect was, I would have to go back to the commune.

"That's very kind of you, but, if I take your car, you'll be stranded here," I pointed out.

Was I secretly hoping that he would volunteer to accompany me? But . . . it would surely be unwise to risk an unpleasant clash between him and Micky?

"I've plenty to do, around the camp. I must try to find out where my mysterious 'cousin' has located himself. I want a word or two with him," Shadrack said purposefully.

"Be careful, then . . . "

"Careful?" His brows quirked upwards. "Of what?"

"I don't know," I said lamely. "To me, he looked rather a tough character. When I tried to induce him to take £40 on account, he growled at me quite threateningly."

"You're a girl. He'll scarcely dare to threaten *me*," Shadrack said loftily. "Probably, he has already made himself scarce, but I'll have to check. We've had a bit of trouble in previous years, with enterprising lads and lassies thinking they can sneak into an empty caravan for a free weekend."

"I suppose you jumped to the conclusion that I'd done just that?" Again, I wished I had insisted on a receipt. "I've no proof that I paid for my accommodation."

"I would doubt if you're that good an actress," he said drily. "One never knows, of course . . . "

I felt myself flushing. Had commonsense prevailed? Was he trying to draw back before he had committed himself to a girl whom he couldn't trust unreservedly? On the face of it, I might well be a dubious character; a far from suitable friend for an upright young accountant.

Or — did he suspect that I was more intimately involved with Micky than I had admitted? He was certain that Micky was a crook. He hadn't attempted to disguise that conviction. My reluctant loyalty to Micky must inevitably make me look like a shady character, too.

"No," I said dully. "You don't know. You're taking a risk in lending me your car."

"Oh, for heaven's sake!" he said in an exasperated tone. "I was joking."

"'Many a true word . . . '" I quoted. "I fancy your subconscious was warning you. One can hardly blame it."

"You're dithering," he accused me. "What's the matter? Afraid to face this Micky fellow? Want me to come with you and hold your hand?"

That was just what I did want, but pride forbade me to admit it.

I jerked up my chin and said coolly: "Good heavens, no! He's perfectly harmless."

7

"**I**'LL be careful," I promised, wriggling the seat forward so that I could reach the pedals more easily. "I have driven Fords before."

Shadrack's car was a Ford Fiesta. In spite of a thick coating of mud, I divined that she was nearly new. In fact, the mile-ometer registered only just over 10,000 miles.

"Good. Take it easily," Shadrack responded.

He had insisted on backing the car out of the garage for me. He was the type of man who didn't believe that any girl could be a competent driver, I decided, perhaps unfairly. Why was I anxious to find flaws in him? Was it a defensive tactic?

The car handled well. Everything worked just as it should, and the tank was almost full. Typical of Shadrack, I fancied. He wouldn't be one of those proud owners who cleaned and polished their cars every weekend, but he would maintain his car in perfect order.

She was fast; surprisingly fast. It would be all too easy to be run in for speeding. Just a light pressure on the accelerator, and one was conscious of a swift surge of power. We swooped and soared over the undulating coast road. The sun was shining fitfully in a sky of rapidly moving, fleecy clouds. The air was fresh and invigorating. I would be enjoying this drive, if it were not for what lay in store for me at the end of it.

After last night's heavy rain, the mud looked deeper and the tents more bedraggled, but basically the commune was unchanged. I left the Fiesta on reasonably firm ground near the entrance and plodded up the worn track to the cobbled yard in front of the converted barn. As usual, a camp fire was burning there, and as usual at midday a big iron pot of stew was steaming over it.

Only on a relentlessly wet day did Greta reluctantly allow members to feed in her kitchen. In fine weather, they were expected to relish camp-fire or barbecue cooking. Some of those luckier members who owned caravans or cabins had Calor gas stoves or rings and could prepare their own meals under cover. The luckless dwellers in tents or in the 'hen roost' would be hard put to it during the winter months, I surmised.

There was the usual motley gathering around the fire, with the usual motley collection of bowls, plates and cutlery. This kind of existence was too untidy and, in the majority of cases, too aimless ever to have appealed to me. What did the untalented and undedicated get out of it? Freedom, Robin had insisted earnestly. Freedom for *what?* I had queried. To be chilly and muddy, ill housed and ill fed?

"Well! Look who's here!" Sharp-eyed, sharp-featured Lettice was the first to notice my approach. There was no pretence of welcome in her tone. "You've a nerve, haven't you?"

"Running to us for shelter now that the cops are on your trail?" Foxy inquired disagreeably. "You're a dark horse, you are!"

"I came to see Micky," I said flatly, scanning the uneven circle for his sleek fair head. "Isn't he here?"

"I fancy he went out to look for you. He was really upset when he read the paper." Booby, flushed and untidy, was spooning out the contents of the iron pot. She waved the ladle at me in a distracted gesture. "Oh, Helen, what have you been doing? Did you grab that woman's jewellery out of revenge, like it hints in the paper?"

"Good heavens, no! I haven't been within a hundred miles of Malbury. You know that. I was here all yesterday morning," I said emphatically.

"Were you?" Booby sounded flustered. "You were here at tea-time when Micky came back, but you weren't here for lunch."

"No. I wasn't. I bought a pasty and some lemonade in the village."

I had been too worked up over Lettice's and her companions' depredations to walk back to the commune with them. I had gone off by myself, to the cliffs. I had found a clump of dry bracken and sat there, munching the pasty and sipping lemonade.

"Can you prove that you weren't in

Malbury?" Greta inquired dispassionately.

"Yes. Of course. I was in the village stores, with Lettice and Foxy and that big man, over there — " I nodded to the burly, bearded youth who was noisily swigging a large bowlful of broth.

"Were you? Odd that we didn't happen to see you," Lettice commented acidly.

"You didn't see me? Oh, nonsense! Of course you did," I protested.

"I didn't," Foxy said blandly. "Did you, Hal?"

The bearded man shook his head. Lettice gave me a spiteful little smile.

"No use trying to hide behind us. We can't give you an alibi," she proclaimed.

"But . . . I walked down to the village with you. There were half a dozen of us. You must remember . . . "

"Not yesterday. You're muddling it with Friday," Foxy said, grinning at me maliciously. "Yesterday, you and Micky disappeared early on, in your car."

"I didn't. Micky went off with Robin."

"Gave me a lift as far as Weymouth," Robin said laconically. "I came back by bus."

"I wasn't with you," I insisted

desperately. "You know that."

"Weren't you? I don't recall," Robin said, shrugging his bony shoulders. "I certainly couldn't swear to it. I was rather under the impression that you'd dropped both of us and driven on alone."

"You know that isn't so — " I stared incredulously at him — and then around the circle. I encountered only blank looks or sly grins, except from Booby, who was looking concerned, and from Greta, who wore an expression of chilly disapproval. "What are you trying to do to me?"

"It's the other way about, surely?" Greta's tone matched her expression. "You're trying to hide yourself here. You're expecting us to shield you. Certainly, the community spirit is what we stand for, but we don't want to get in wrong with the police. You've no right to ask us to lie on your behalf."

"That's the last thing I'd ask anyone to do. On the contrary, I'm asking you to tell the truth," I flashed.

"You're not really one of us. You were merely making use of us for a cheap holiday," Greta went on severely, as if I hadn't spoken. "You didn't fit in, from

118

the first. Micky shouldn't have brought you here, but obviously you'd played on his sympathies."

"Wrongful dismissal?" Lettice's lips curled. "You should read what that Forrester woman has to say about you and your filthy temper."

"Oh, Cos, don't! I'm sure Helen didn't mean to be brutal," Booby interposed, in her good-natured, blundering fashion. "Here's a spare bowl! Have some broth, Helen."

Reluctantly, I sat down beside Booby. There didn't appear to be anything else to do. I had to see Micky. He would stand by me, surely? Whether he had been to Malbury or not, he knew I hadn't.

The others knew that, too, of course. They were exacting a petty revenge on me, for what they considered my prim and censorious attitude, by pretending that I hadn't been down to the village with them. Surely Micky would compel them to tell the truth? Micky wouldn't join in any conspiracy against me.

The broth contrived to be both greasy and watery. Lumps of partially cooked parsnips and potatoes and carrots failed to make it palatable, and I nearly broke a tooth on a piece of mutton bone.

The conversation around the fire was like the humming of a hive of bees, as far as I was concerned . . . muffled and unintelligible. I was being purposefully excluded from it, I realised. Booby, beside me, was obviously aware of my isolation. She kept on casting uneasy, half-guilty glances at me.

"You are all right, Helen?" she ventured, when I put down my still half-full bowl. "I felt awful about you after you'd gone. I mean, if you'd collapsed, all on your own, you might have had a horrid accident."

There was genuine concern in her tone. I blinked at her.

"Collapse? Why on earth should I collapse?" I asked blankly.

"People do. In your condition, I mean," she mumbled.

"What condition?"

She cast a furtive look around and then spoke in a hoarse whisper.

"Cos said you were expecting a baby."

"I? Good heavens!" I said limply.

"Whatever gave her that crack-brained notion?"

"Because . . . " Booby swallowed audibly. "You wouldn't share Micky's tent. Remember? Yet he seemed to feel responsible for you. Why else did he bring you here?"

"He professed to be in love with me," I said drily. "Lettice is right off the target in her surmises."

"Oh? Well, that's a good thing, isn't it?" Booby said — as if she were unsure. "But . . . why did you come back? If you haven't any claim on Micky . . . "

"I needed to ask him some pertinent questions. He borrowed my car yesterday. Where did he take it? To Malbury?"

"Oh, Helen!" She opened her eyes very wide. "You can't think Micky's a thief?"

"No. Of course not," I said hastily.

Impossible to put into concise words what I thought or felt about Micky Harris. The picture was badly blurred, as if it had been left out in the rain overnight. All I was sure of was that I had to see him again; had to question him.

Yet when, as I was sipping a mug of

singularly tasteless coffee, he came roaring into the yard on a sleek looking motor bicycle, my first impulse was towards flight. He was too high-powered for me, I thought confusedly.

Dismounted, and removing his crash helmet, Micky conveyed the impression of a professional actor, about to step confidently on to the stage to play his part in a successful production. Fair head poised, he sent his brillant, blue-eyed gaze flashing around the assembly. Then, in a very few strides, he was beside me, exclaiming: "Curly! Oh, this is grand!" on a jubilant note. "Darling girl, you've come back!"

"Not I. This is just my ghost . . . " the tart response came unbidden from my lips.

Micky laughed in a half-hearted fashion and reached for my hands. The gesture was ruined, because I was still clasping the mug of lukewarm coffee. The mug tilted and the muddy fluid spilt across the back of one of his hands. He made a moue of distaste and took the mug from me, to dump it on the cobbles.

"Curly, sweetest," he began again.

"This is a relief. I've been madly worried about you."

"Have you? Why?"

"Rushing off like that," he said reproachfully. "I'd no idea where you were going. Anything could have happened to you."

"You should have known that I wouldn't get far. You forgot to fill up the petrol tank."

"Oh, no! Did I? How stupid of me! Sorry," he said, looking entirely unabashed. "I hope you weren't stranded?"

"Not entirely. I found accommodation."

"Oh, good! Where?"

"That's of no importance."

We sounded unnaturally stiff and stilted. I supposed that we were both aware that Booby wasn't the only person who was openly listening to us.

"You came back . . . "

"Because I had to talk to you . . . "

"Well, then — " With less than his usual grace, Micky scrambled to his feet and pulled me up, beside him. "Let's take a stroll."

Somebody sniggered and I felt my skin burning. I thought inconsequently that, had Micky not brought me here, had he instead taken me to an impersonal holiday camp like Shadrack's uncle's, our embryo romance might have survived. It hadn't been robust enough to survive contact with the Down to Earthers.

I said impulsively: "Your friends really are an unpleasant crowd."

"Most are harmless and friendly enough. You just happened to ruffle the feathers of the unpleasant minority," he retorted. "Why let them ruffle yours?"

"They're spiteful. Positively malicious. Lettice told Booby that I was pregnant," I said indignantly.

"You're not, are you? Then — why worry?" He essayed an airy laugh. "The trouble with you, Curly love, is that you take everyone and everything a mite too seriously."

"Possibly. Foolish of me, isn't it? I even took *you* seriously."

"That's different. No need for sarcasm. I am serious, where you're concerned."

He sounded sober and sincere. I didn't know whether to believe him or not. It couldn't make any great difference, either way, except to my hurt pride. It would be gratifying to my pride to be convinced that Micky cared something for me.

He was still holding my hand. He gave it an affectionate squeeze.

"You came back," he reminded me.

"Yes. To ask you about my car." I let my fingers lie limply in his. I wasn't going to make a production of wrenching them free. "Did you take the car to Malbury yesterday?"

"To Malbury?" His tone was one of genuine astonishment. "Hell, no! Why would I?"

"Haven't you read today's newspapers?"

"As a matter of fact, no. They hadn't arrived here when I took off to look for you."

"Then you didn't know that Millicent Forrester had been robbed?"

"Forrester? That woman you were working for, d'you mean?"

"Who else? Someone walked into High Rise whilst she was at a gymkhana with young Caroline. She appears to imagine that it was I or one of my boyfriends."

"Heavens!"

He couldn't be acting, I told myself hopefully. He was truly flabbergasted.

125

"Easy enough to prove that you were nowhere near," he added reassuringly.

"I wasn't, but, apparently, the Peugeot was. Where did you take her, Micky?"

"Hither and thither, but not out of Dorset," his reply came promptly. He squeezed my fingers again. "Silly love! Did you suspect me of ransacking High Rise? Shame on you!"

"No. I didn't suspect you. Not really," I answered awkwardly. "Only — it is odd about the Peugeot. She was reported as having been near High Rise, and the police are looking for her."

"A mistake, obviously. Eye-witnesses rarely get makes and registration numbers correctly. Don't let it worry you!" Micky said easily.

"N-no . . . except that my car ought to have been readily identifiable by the locals. Can you prove that you didn't cross the Devon border yesterday?"

"Probably. If I must. Where's the car now?"

"I've no idea. Someone has borrowed her."

"When? Where?"

"From where I'd left her parked

126

overnight. Farther along the coast."

I was oddly reluctant to disclose the caravan's whereabouts. Micky frowned.

"Why the secrecy? Trying to elude me? Or — to incite me?"

"Enough is enough. It was a mistake to come here with you. That kind of mistake is better forgotten."

"In whose opinion? I didn't make any mistake about *you*, Curly. I'm still dead keen." He gave me one of his ice-melting glances. "Don't tell me you've changed. I refuse to believe it. We have something pretty good going for us."

"We thought we did. It simply hasn't worked out," I said flatly. "Sorry, Micky!"

"Sorry? Is that all you have to say?" His fair skin was reddening. "You are the most maddeningly elusive creature. What's the big idea? Haven't I been patient and long-suffering and danced to your tune? A nice fool you made me look, too, when you dashed off last night!"

"I'm sorry," I repeated lamely. "You have been kind."

"Kind?" he echoed scornfully. "I'm

beginning to wonder. Could be that this was a put-up job all along — and you played me for a sucker."

"What on earth d'you mean?"

"Maybe you did give a boy-friend a spare key to High Rise — to be used when you were safely out of the way. Maybe you were using me as a smoke-screen."

"That's nonsense! After you and I started dating, I didn't have any other male friends."

"No? What about Sydney?"

"Samantha's friend. Not mine."

He was walking fast now, pulling me along with him, up the muddy path round the big barn towards the stunted copse behind it. The hum of voices round the fire died away. The only sounds were Micky's quickened breathing and a faint rustling from the dead or dying leaves on the wind-swept trees.

I was becoming acutely conscious of Micky's tight clasp and of the anger seething in him; anger heightened by frustration. I felt wretchedly guilty — but of what? If I had 'encouraged' Micky, I had also 'encouraged' myself. I had hoped most sincerely that he was the man for me. I had wanted him to love me, yes. I had almost persuaded myself that I loved him.

We plunged into the copse. The dead leaves were soggy under our feet. Only a few recently fallen leaves crackled pleasantly as we trod on them. I had always loved walking through dry, rustling leaves, I remembered inconsequently. There were giant horse-chestnut trees beyond the lawn, at the bottom of the Rectory garden. How many hours had I spent in my childhood, fishing about among those crisp, crackling leaves and pouncing triumphantly on the richly glowing horse-chestnuts?

"Did you collect conkers when you were a child?" I asked abruptly.

"Conkers? What the dickens are conkers?" Micky retorted, frowning again.

"You don't know?"

I was appalled; to a ridiculous extent. It was as if a deep chasm had opened between us.

"Helen!" He stopped short and swung me round to face him. "Stop it!"

"What?"

"Stop playing games . . . being purposely elusive, and provocative. I've had enough of it. Be honest with me!"

"Yes. Yes, of course."

"There's no 'of course' about it. You've been deliberately tantalising me. Now — tell me the truth. Why did you bolt off last night? And why have you come back now?"

"Yesterday surely explains itself. I couldn't have stayed on, after that horrid scene. It was quite clear that I wasn't welcome."

"Who created the said horrid scene? You brought it about, purposely. All that fuss about a few tins of soup!"

"Stolen tins . . . "

"You didn't raise the point until it suited you," he assured me. "You must have suspected all along that some of the commune members poached or pinched their contributions to the grub."

"I guessed about the poaching, yes. Not about the filching from village stores," I said defensively. "I hadn't guessed that you would back up the shoplifters."

"I didn't. I merely didn't consider it my business — or yours. The rule is

130

that everyone contributes towards the main meals in his or her turn. How, is a member's own affair."

"Yes? You made your point yesterday evening. I couldn't go along with it."

"A trumped-up excuse for walking out on me!"

"No. A basic issue. Micky, please try to understand. We had been good friends, and I had hoped for — well, for something more. Ever since we left Plymouth, I had been reluctantly realising that we had made a mistake."

"Speak for yourself!"

"All right, then. I had made a mistake. So — the only thing to do seemed to be to cut the loss."

"With an airy 'Thanks for the memory!'? Not good enough, Curly!"

He let go of my hand so suddenly that I staggered back against a tree-trunk. Before I could regain my balance, he had both arms around me. He was holding me to him in a crushing embrace. I tried to jerk my head back, but I couldn't avoid those eager, searching lips. He was kissing me as if out to make a meal of me.

I didn't struggle. I realised that it would be useless to resist this onslaught; that any such attempt would merely incite him. I didn't, in actual fact, feel any sense of revulsion. He was an attractive man. I hadn't been wrong about that. His fair, clean-shaven skin didn't rasp mine, and his lips hadn't that hotly moist, octopus-like suction which I had always found repulsive.

I stood there passively, my main emotion one of regret. There was so much about the man that appealed to me. I admired his good looks and careful grooming. I liked the regularity of his features, the texture of his skin, and his deft, well-kept hands. He had been a delightful escort. He had never harassed, embarrassed, or bored me. If I had stayed on at High Rise, I should have gone on looking forward to my dates, thinking of him fondly, and dreaming of a joint future.

"If only — " but as my mother was wont to say in her practical fashion, life was made up of 'if onlys . . . ' some causes of bitter remorse and others of supreme thankfulness.

"You do care about me!" he exclaimed, huskily and triumphantly, raising his head at last to take a deep breath. "You like being kissed by me. You can't deny it."

"I think most girls would like it. You kiss very well. No fumbling or slobbering."

At that, he gave me a sudden shake.

"Now you're trying to provoke me again! You maddening creature, you! How the hell does one get under your skin? It's like an elephant's hide."

"I hope not. That would be a poor recommendation for the skin-cream I use."

"Making fun of me now, is she? Honestly, Curly, you're the kind of girl who asks to be murdered," he said in exasperation.

"Then you've had a fortunate escape, haven't you? I'm truly sorry, Micky," I said, noting with some compunction the sweat on his brow and upper lip. "I'm not good with men. I do recognise that. They like the look of me, but I always seem to end up by irritating them."

"Irritating?" he echoed. "You should have heard your friend, Sydney, on the

133

subject! What wouldn't he relish doing to that insufferably stuck-up little so-and-so? Throttling was about his kindest suggestion."

"You're making it up, Micky. I can't imagine Sydney's saying 'insufferable'. And . . . he was never a friend of mine."

"That's the whole point. He wouldn't say 'insufferable', but *you* would." He put his sleek fair head on one side and raked me with his brilliant blue-eyed gaze. "I suppose it didn't dawn on you that, in those foursomes Samantha arranged, Sydney was included for your benefit?"

"For mine? Oh, no."

"Oh, yes! But . . . little Miss Disdain had no use for him, had she? Instead, she calmly annexed her girl friend's heart-throb." He gave me a lop-sided grin. "'How to make friends and influence people'. You do seek to endear yourself to lesser females, don't you?"

"Oh, Micky, no! I didn't know. Samantha should have warned me," I protested.

"Would that have made any difference? Would you have respected her 'Hands off that man — '? I wonder!"

"I wouldn't have poached."

"No? Maybe, you couldn't have helped it. The damage was done the first time you smiled at me," he said flatly. "Samantha didn't stand an earthly after that."

"Drop it, Micky! You're making me sound like some kind of siren, and I'm anything but. I told you. My romances always peter out or get frosted in the bud. I haven't the knack of managing men."

"With your looks and your ingenuous approach, you don't need it."

"I do. At least, I need something. A setting agent, perhaps, like pectin for jams," I said vaguely. "It's so disappointing, when you've done every-thing you should, and a jam just won't set."

"*Jam?* Who's talking about jam?" Micky demanded blankly.

"That's how it looks to me. Mostly, the jams and jellies I've made have set very well, but I have had the occasional failure," I tried to explain. "With the men I meet, the pectin just isn't there.

I suppose there's something lacking in me."

"Or deliberately withheld. It's odd, because you don't look frigid."

"Frigid? Oh, no! I'm not. I'm sure I'm not."

"Then, why? Why don't you respond to a fellow?" Again, he gave me a shake. "You don't resist and you don't respond. What the hell is one to make of you?"

"I don't know. I simply do not know," I admitted unhappily. "Worrying, isn't it?"

"You can say that again!"

8

"IF the eye-witnesses insist that the Peugeot was in Malbury yesterday, and you can't prove that it wasn't, we shall have some awkward questions to answer," I said apprehensively. "Lettice and Foxy and Hal are flatly refusing to admit that I was in the village stores with them. Mrs Hickson might remember me, but I wouldn't like to count on her. The little shop was crowded."

"Would you expect that trio to give you an alibi? Haven't you even noticed the way Foxy has been eyeing you? If you were a game bird, he'd have his nets out for you," Micky said meaningly.

"That awful man! No, I certainly hadn't noticed. I know Lettice dislikes me. It's mutual," I said frankly. "Surely she can't imagine that I would look twice at her poacher friend?"

"That's probably another score against you, from her point of view," he warned me. "We shall have to hope that someone will remember having seen your car in Weymouth or Dorchester. The parking tickets should be still on the windscreen, unless you've removed them."

"I haven't. I didn't even notice them. You were in Weymouth and Dorchester?"

"Certainly." He paused, then looked at me challengingly. "Why don't you believe me?"

"I do. Of course, I do."

What reason had I to doubt his word? Had I ever caught him out in a deliberate lie? Not that I could recall. He might embroider facts, but he wasn't a downright liar. I could have been confident that he wasn't a thief, either, if it hadn't been for that diamond ring.

The memory of that ring was like a thorn, festering under my skin. I ought to tackle Micky about it. Why did I hesitate? Because there was simply no tactful way of putting that particular question. However I voiced it, it would be tantamount to an accusation.

I didn't, I realised, want to break with Micky in that way; a way which would inevitably leave a bitter taste in our throats. I might not love him, but I did have this affection for him. I looked regretfully at his clean-cut profile, at his shining fair hair, and his slim, elegant figure. I would have liked to keep him as a friend.

"Then, where's the problem? Why are you worrying? Obviously, whoever reported the car's presence in Malbury made a mistake in the registration number," Micky said impatiently.

"I could accept that if my car was a Mini or a Ford, but small yellow Peugeots aren't all that common. It seems too great a coincidence," I said unhappily.

"You can't take my word for it? When have I ever lied to you?" he demanded reproachfully.

"I don't know. Please, Micky, don't be vexed with me!"

"Vexed? Oh, Curly, you're impossible!"

We had been sauntering away from the shelter of the trees, slowly, as if mutually reluctant to end our exchange, and yet as if accepting the inevitable. Abruptly, Micky reached out for me again, as if only through physical contact could we communicate intelligibly.

He held me close to him, his fingers digging into my arms. I was aware of his quickened breathing and swift heart-beats. Yes, I could stir him . . . could make his blood race . . . and yet there was this invisible barrier between us.

"I love you," he said in an oddly strained tone. "I didn't think I'd ever say that — and mean it — to any girl, but there's something about you, maddening though you are, that I can't resist."

"Well, thank you," I said lamely. "That's very sweet of you, Micky."

"Hell! Is that your only response?"

"What more can I say? I am grateful . . . "

"*Grateful?* Who wants gratitude?"

I groaned inwardly. Before I had left Malbury, I had been yearning for Micky to commit himself. I had long had a horror of becoming a victim of unrequited love. I had resolved, early on in my 'teens, that I would never let myself love a man unless I was certain that he loved me.

In Malbury, Micky had been affectionate, but elusive. He had paid me extravagant tributes, but he had refrained from using those three inimitable words 'I love you'.

Three weeks — or less — ago, they would have been music in my ears. Now they were as embarrassing as a costly, unexpected and unwanted gift.

"I could have sworn that you were keen on me," he went on, his voice roughening. "Why have you changed?"

"Have I? Perhaps. I don't know . . . "

"There isn't anyone else? No, there can't be. You were pretty cool towards all the fellows here," he said, as if thinking aloud. Then, his eyes narrowed. "You're flushing . . . looking guilty. There is another fellow. Who?"

I shook my head.

"It wouldn't work, Micky. I saw that, when I was here. The pectin was missing."

"You don't trust me. That's the truth of it," he said, still in that roughened tone which was such a contrast to his usual cool serenity. "Hell! Why did this have to happen to me? I was ready to go the whole way for you. I'd even bought a ring."

"You'd bought a ring?" The words came out in a startled gasp. "A diamond ring?"

141

"Yes. How did you know?"

"Show me!"

"I can't. You'll never believe this one, but I lost it." His colour rose just perceptibly. "Fact is, it wasn't brand new. I bought it from a friend. I was going to get a proper box for it, from a jeweller's. I had it in my anorak pocket, wrapped in a handkerchief. I must have pulled out the handkerchief somewhere or other, forgetting about the ring. Damn' fool thing to do . . . "

"I found it," I said awkwardly. "It had rolled into a corner of the Peugeot's boot."

"Well, that's a bit of luck! Why didn't you say so? Where is it?"

There was a moment's strained silence, in which I struggled vainly for an adequate reason to produce for having concealed the ring. With his brilliant, probing gaze on me, I remained helplessly tongue-tied, while his clear-cut features hardened, like fast-setting concrete.

"You thought there was something fishy about it? I see!" he said coldly. "Maybe, you jumped to the conclusion that it belonged to your ex-employer?"

142

"It could have been hers. She had one exactly like it. I'm sorry, Micky," I said unhappily. "I simply didn't know what to think or what to do with the ring."

"Why didn't you take it to the police?"

"How could I? After those dark hints Mrs Forrester dropped about me to the Sunday Spotlight, I daren't go near the police. Besides . . . " I swallowed hard. "Honestly and truly, Micky, I couldn't believe that you had robbed Mrs Forrester. It just wasn't your style."

"I suppose that's something — " but his expression was still bleak. "It didn't occur to you that I might have bought the ring for you?"

"I'm afraid it didn't. Because it was loose. If it had been in a jeweller's box — "

"I should have had to pay around twice as much for it, had I gone to a jeweller's shop," he said candidly. "This fellow I know deals in jewellery wholesale, and also in the 'nearly new'. I mean, a chap buys an engagement ring and then the engagement is called off and he gets the ring back. What's he to do with it? Probably, the jeweller from whom

143

he bought it won't give him a decent price, even though the ring has hardly been worn."

I smiled involuntarily. The explanation seemed typical of Micky. He had a keen sense of values. He liked the best, but he would always acquire it at cost price, if he could. To buy a 'scarcely worn' ring at a bargain price would appeal to him as a shrewd deal. Financially, no doubt, it was. Emotionally? I wouldn't have wanted the symbol of some other girl's ill-fated romance, however much of a bargain or however good an investment.

"It was virtually new. If I'd given it to you in a jeweller's box, you would never have guessed that it had ever been worn," Micky persisted. "No need to look like that."

"'What the eye doesn't see . . . '" I quoted. "I dare say you're right."

Only, the gesture would have typified the gulf between us, I reasoned confusedly. Micky would always feel justified in deceiving a girl — even the girl he was serious about — for her own peace of mind. Shadrack wouldn't. That thought flashed unbidden into my head.

If Shadrack acquired a ring second-hand, he wouldn't attempt to conceal the fact.

If? Perhaps it should be 'if ever'. He didn't appear to be in a hurry to pledge himself to any of his girl friends. Few young men were in these days, when girls bestowed themselves so freely and lavishly, without yearning for security or permanence.

"Marriage? Not for me, thank you!" Samantha had insisted. "All very fine if you can be certain that the man's in the money. Otherwise, a girl's likely to find herself working to support her husband and kids. Men are more often made redundant than we are. Syd's had half a dozen different jobs since I first met him."

"Well, then — " Micky's handsome features wore a perplexed air. "Where's the problem? Pop the ring on your finger, and we're all set."

"All set?" For what? Wedding bells? The traditional 'happy ending'? Couldn't he see that it was too late for that?

As I hesitated, he asked sharply: "Where is the ring? You haven't lost it? I paid a hundred smackers for it."

"Oh, Micky!" Again, I was conscious of the gulf between us. "You could have bought a nice, brand-new ring for £50."

"Not diamonds. Not of that calibre. Would you expect me to give you topaz or garnets?"

"I like both. I prefer coloured stones."

"Don't be difficult, Curly love! Where is the ring?"

"I hid it," I had to admit. "It's quite safe."

"That's a mercy!" He cleared his throat. "See here, if it honestly doesn't appeal to you, I'll trade it in for something else."

That touched me more than any impassioned pleading. If Micky was ready to forfeit a red-hot bargain on my account, he must have a genuine affection for me. It seemed a great pity that I couldn't respond.

I said: "You're a dear, Micky. I wish — I really do wish — that I was in love with you — " and he made a grimace at me.

"I'm beginning to wonder if you're capable of falling in love," he said acidly.

"Oh, I hope I am! It would be grim if I never did fall in love. Honestly, in Malbury I did think I loved you," I said regretfully.

"Couldn't you think that way again? Will you try?"

"I doubt if trying would be any good. I'm sorry, Micky. It might have been nice to have had a husband other girls would have envied me. Or, of course, it might have been uncomfortable and embarrassing. I suppose it would have depended on your reactions."

"Oh, you're hopeless! Are you out to provoke me beyond endurance?"

"Sorry," I said again. "I'd better go now."

"Go — where? Why this caginess about where you're staying?"

"Various reasons," I said evasively.

"Such as?"

"Someone has it in for me. Apart from your friends here, I mean. I shall feel safer if nobody knows where to reach me."

"Evidently, you *don't* trust me," he said, on an aggrieved note. "That hurts."

"I don't — I can't — trust your

friends," I said candidly. "If you'll promise not to tell them — "

Instinct was warning me to keep my address to myself, but I couldn't help feeling guilty about Micky. I had hurt him. He was making that abundantly clear. I hated the thought of hurting anyone, even inadvertently — and I was by no means indifferent to Micky. He did care about me, even to the extent of buying a diamond ring for me. He wouldn't willingly involve me in trouble. I was confident of that.

"I won't tell a soul," he vowed. "And that includes the fuzz."

"Thanks! There's another reason, actually, for keeping quiet about my accommodation. I've hired a caravan in a camp which is officially closed till next Easter."

"Oh! I get you," he said in obvious relief. "A deal on the side?"

That, he could readily understand, I reflected, with a pang. 'Side deals', not strictly illegal, but not strictly according to the rules, either, were a part of his world. 'Wheeling and dealing' was the accepted phrase, wasn't it? He wouldn't stick his neck out far enough to handle goods from hi-jacked lorries, because he was determined to keep on the right side of the law, but he wouldn't hesitate to make a profit on goods from a firm forced into bankruptcy or on goods from fire- or flood-damaged warehouses. He was rather like a sparrow — no, a perky, bold-eyed robin — seeking out and snatching up palatable scraps as and when he could spot them.

"A bit grim, I would think," he added doubtfully. "You're in a deserted camp?"

I nodded. I was curiously reluctant to mention Shadrack.

"I ran out of petrol, since you'd forgotten to top up the tank. It was a case of 'any port in a storm' last night," I said wryly. "It's not exactly isolated. There are neighbours, and someone connected with the Heatherview Camp let me hire the caravan. I've paid for the week."

"The Heatherview? That's a new one on me. Where, exactly, is it located?"

"Down a turning off the coastal road."

"That's very explicit! Which is the nearest town or village?"

"I'm not sure. I suppose it must be Abbotsbury."

"The other side of Weymouth, then? Why? Were you heading back to Devon?" he asked in patent surprise.

"I didn't stop to think. I simply wanted to get away. I hadn't any real reason for taking any particular route," I admitted.

"I still can't imagine why you felt compelled to rush away," he grumbled.

"That's just it! I mean, there's the gulf between us," I said regretfully. "You couldn't see why . . . "

"Love can bridge any gulf," he said, with his familiar air of producing a cliché as though it were an original discovery.

"I doubt it. I very much doubt it. Some gulfs are too wide for bridges. I do like firm ground under my feet," I told him. "I wouldn't have the nerve to cross a deep chasm by one of those swaying rope bridges you see in adventure films. I should stick halfway, if I ever could force myself to attempt it."

"You're impossible!" he said again, in patent exasperation — and I answered: "This is where we came in, Micky. Let me go now, please!"

"Can I stop you?"

He mooched along beside me, hands in pockets, his normally jaunty air in abeyance. Was he trying to make me feel guilty? Neither a sense of guilt nor a sense of gratitude could bring us any closer together. I was uncomfortably certain of that.

The circle round the camp fire had broken up, but a few of the Down to Earthers remained, lounging there over mugs of coffee or cigarettes. Smoking, unless it was of home-grown, herbal mixtures, was frowned upon by Greta and Jacko as 'pollution', but Lettice and Foxy, amongst others, were compulsive smokers. They were sprawled close together on a tattered rug. I could feel their malignant glances on us, as we made our way across the yard.

"That girl loathes me," I said, under my breath.

"Cos? You shouldn't let her rile you. She's quite a good kid, really. A bit of a spoilt brat, of course, but sound at heart," Micky said defensively. "She's simply jealous. That's all."

"Jealous? Of me? Why?" I asked

blankly — and he smiled self-consciously. "Because of *you*? I thought Foxy was her boy-friend."

"He is . . . now. I used to be. Briefly. Before I met you, Curly love."

"I see."

There didn't appear to be anything I could add to that. I quickened my steps towards the Fiesta.

"Where's your Peugeot?" Micky inquired.

"I wish I knew! Someone appears to have borrowed it."

"Someone? Who?"

"How do I know? I had to borrow this Fiesta to get here."

"Whose car is it?" he demanded.

"Oh, really, Micky! Is that of any importance? It's a neighbour's . . . " I hoped devoutly that I wasn't flushing, but I felt hot and harassed and still absurdly guilty. Once again, my one impulse was to escape from this place as swiftly as I could.

Perkin was sitting bolt upright in the passenger's seat. He greeted me with reproachful whimpers. I had to let him out on the grass for a brief run around, and Micky seized the chance to renew his attack.

"If you're hoping to wear me down, forget it!" I snapped, exasperated. "When people try to push me around, I can be as stubborn as any donkey. You should know that by now."

"I can be determined, too . . . "

He made an ominous move forward as if he would clasp me to him again. Mercifully, for me, Perkin chose that moment to make friendly, puppyish advances, and pawed at one of Micky's immaculately creased, pale grey trouser legs, leaving two large, muddy imprints.

Micky stepped back hastily with a muttered imprecation, and I bundled Perkin and myself into the Fiesta. To my relief, the engine fired at a touch and we shot away, slithering on the slimy ground.

"Thanks, pal!" I said gratefully, and patted the softly silky head beside me.

9

"SHADRACK!" I called. "*Shadrack!*"
There was no answer. Tentatively, I turned the door handle — to discover that the door was locked. I felt quite unreasonably disappointed. There had been no compulsion on Shadrack to wait around for my return. He had, in fact, warned me that he would be busy. Yet, somehow, I had expected him to be here to welcome me, eager to learn the result of my trip, and glad to see me safely back at the camp.

Trying to stifle a let-down feeling, I asked myself defiantly why he should care? What could I possibly mean to him? Obviously, he wasn't worried about his car. That was a tribute to me. Or, of course, he could have been called away.

I was annoyed that I should feel so disconsolate. Hadn't I learnt a lesson over Micky? It was stupid to rely on a man. It was inviting disillusionment, if nothing more painful. Why couldn't I be content to go it alone?

I should, I supposed, leave Shadrack's car here for him but, in a perverse mood, I got back behind the wheel and drove down to my caravan. If he wanted his car, he could jolly well fetch it.

The caravan, which had seemed a blessed refuge last night, now looked cramped and uninviting. I wrinkled up my nostrils distastefully. The air had a stale, unpleasing smell to it. A smell of carelessly stubbed-out cigarettes, cheap perfume and human sweat? But . . . how was that possible? I didn't smoke or use cheap scent, and I had been far too chilled last night to sweat.

I hastily opened a window. Perkin was pawing at my ankles. Poor scrap! He must be feeling a bit neglected. I stooped to pat him — and saw the filter-tip stubs on the floor. There were two of them. One was the smallest of stubs. The other was of a half-smoked cigarette and the filter tip was faintly coloured, as if the smoker had been using one of those pale lipsticks.

I felt my nerves jerking in reaction. I tried to reason that the stubs must have been on the floor last night. I simply hadn't had occasion to notice them. I couldn't convince myself. I might have overlooked the stubs. I couldn't have been insensitive to the reek of stale tobacco and that sickly perfume. Someone — probably two people — had been in the caravan recently. Who? Not Shadrack. He wouldn't have taken advantage of my absence to search my belongings. Or — would he?

How much — or rather how little — did I know about the man? Why had I believed his account of himself so readily? He, not that first bearded 'nephew', might be the intruder.

No. Shadrack must be authentic. Shadrack had the keys to the bungalow, and was obviously at home there. Then he would have a master key to the caravans, too. He could have unlocked this caravan.

Yes, but he wouldn't have left those stubs. He wouldn't have dropped a cigarette on the floor and trodden on it. Whatever he was or wasn't, I was certain that he wasn't slovenly. Besides, he wouldn't have a girl friend who used that kind of would-be seductive perfume. He had more discrimination.

The puppy was making plaintive sounds. Hungry, poor boy? Puppies ought to have regular and frequent meals, I seemed to recall. Watched hopefully by those velvet brown eyes, I opened a tin of steak and ladled out a generous helping. If Perkin grew to the size indicated by his large, floppy paws, he would cost quite a lot to feed, as Greta had warned me. So — ? I could spend my money as I pleased, couldn't I? That was, if I had any. I might well be out of a job, thanks to Mrs Forrester.

I hadn't needed to enact a petty revenge on Millicent Forrester for sacking me. She had brought retribution on herself. Had I still been with her, I should have escorted Caroline to the gymkhana, and the house wouldn't have been left unoccupied. The thief or thieves would scarcely have walked in had Mrs Forrester remained at home. Had she thought of that? I wondered. Perhaps, once her initial indignation had subsided, she wouldn't greatly regret the loss of the 'material possessions' she had affected to despise.

Perhaps she would prefer to have the insurance money.

Thinking of the missing jewellery, I remembered Micky's ring. I would have to take it — or post it — to him tomorrow. It was a nasty shock to find that the ring had vanished. It confirmed my suspicions that a female had visited the caravan in my absence. A man wouldn't have dreamt of ransacking my sponge-bag for valuables, I was certain.

Apart from the loss, which would inevitably be a nasty blow to Micky, who could scarcely have had time to insure the ring, I felt sore about this invasion. Wasn't it galling enough that someone had borrowed my cherished car? To have unknown, predatory hands exploring my belongings was even worse. Whose hands? That bearded pseudo-nephew's and an accomplice's? He, at least, should have known that I hadn't any spare cash. I had told him so plainly last night. What then, could they have been expecting to find?

Shadrack might have looked for proof of my identity, but he wouldn't have searched my sponge-bag or dropped those stubs on the floor. What had I blundered into here? A den of thieves? Or smugglers? My impulse was for flight, but I had to check it. I couldn't run off in a borrowed car and without any money, on a Sunday evening. I would have to stay put until tomorrow morning. Besides, I needed to see Shadrack again. It was high time I tried to check up on his account of himself.

Could he have been making a fool of me? My self-confidence, which had already taken a hammering, was protesting feebly that I hadn't been misled again. Shadrack had rung true.

Confound it, where could the man be? Had he grown weary of waiting for me and wandered off to the reed-beds again? The light was beginning to dim. From the caravan steps, I could see flocks of birds heading for the marshy ground. Only starlings, I surmised, but possibly rarer birds, too, slept somewhere among those reeds.

Perkin was pushing his empty dish around the floor. It was time he had a walk. I could take him down on the beach. If Shadrack was there, he wouldn't have to know that I'd come looking for him. Perkin would provide an unshakable reason for my presence.

I bundled the pup back into the car and headed out of the camp. The road to the beach was longer than I had anticipated. It wound this way and that, past a couple of farms, clustered cottages, and a few modern looking bungalows, before it finally petered out in a small, deserted carpark. The carpark had railings on the seaward side, and was raised above the beach, but waves were breaking over the railings in clouds of spray. It was a curiously desolate scene, with all those empty, white-lined slots.

I left the Fiesta just inside the entrance, well back from the flying spray. I snapped on Perkin's lead, and we started off along the rough path beside the reed-bed. Perkin signified his approval by tugging on the lead and trotting with tail high and nose to the ground. He was quite strong for so young a pup. He pulled me along at a smart pace, regardless of puddles and potholes.

I would have to teach him to heel, I realised, but I was in no mood for dog training this evening. I had too many other problems on my mind, including the disappearance of Micky's ring. Perhaps that should have been my primary concern, but I was more worried about the whereabouts of the Peugeot — and of Shadrack.

A chilly breeze was blowing off the sea. Quite a strong breeze. It ruffled Perkin's soft coat and my thick curls. Hair was blown over my eyes and across my face. I stopped to fish a head-scarf out of my pocket. As I was struggling to fasten it over my hair, Perkin gave a sudden jerk and his lead slipped through my fingers.

"Wait! Perkin, *wait!*" I commanded and grabbed for the lead. He was too quick for me. He was off into the reeds in a flash. In pursuit of some quarry invisible to me? Or just out of puppy spirits?

I called him imperatively. I finished fastening my scarf and plunged into the reeds after him. They seemed to close round me, whipping at my face and hands. There was no sign of the pup. No sound, either.

"Hell!" I said crossly. "Now, what do I do? Perkin, come! Good boy, Perkin!"

I blundered back on to the path, calling repeatedly. I tried the voice of command — of rising anger. Then, thinking he might be afraid of punishment, I forced myself to use a coaxing, an entreating, and loving tone.

No result. Perkin had vanished. I strained my ears, hoping to hear a rustling, which would indicate where he was exploring. No sound, except the surge of the waves.

Confound that stupid little puppy! Was this his idea of gratitude? I'd saved his life, hadn't I? In the teeth of opposition and censure, I had made myself responsible for him. Yet, the first time he'd had a chance, he had bolted away from me. It would serve him right if I drove off and left him here. He didn't deserve my care and affection. Why on earth should I stand here, shivering, and working myself up about him?

I was hurt and indignant and furiously angry. I was angry with Shadrack for not having been around, so that I needn't have gone in search of him. I was angry with Perkin for his ingratitude. I was angry with myself for having let go of the lead.

I swung away from the reeds. I marched back towards the Fiesta. If Perkin didn't choose to follow me, he could stay where he was. Why should I care? I wouldn't even look back until I had reached the car. Then I turned — but there was no eager bundle of fur loping after me. So what? Good riddance! Greta would say. It wasn't even as if I wanted a dog. Any dog — particularly a large one — would be a handicap in my job. I'd done my best for the pup. Now I could wash my hands of him.

Only . . . of course, I couldn't. I had vivid mental pictures of him . . . of his helpless bewilderment and desolation, if he emerged from the reeds to find that I and the car had gone. What would he do? Where would he roam? He might run blindly up the road and get knocked down by a car. He couldn't, at his age, have any sense of direction — or any common-sense, either.

He would be cold and hungry and frightened. He wouldn't realise that he had brought his abandonment on himself. How could he? He would suffer dumbly without knowing why.

Perhaps he wouldn't even get clear of the reeds. His trailing lead might easily get caught up among those stiff stems. He might be held there, a helpless prisoner. Or — he might plunge in too far and land in deep mud or water. He might not be able to struggle clear. He would drown . . . or starve to death.

I had to find him. There was no alternative. Torn by anxiety and feeling wretchedly helpless, I hurried back to the place where I'd last seen Perkin. At least, I thought it was the place, but how could I be sure? The reeds were swinging in the breeze, every clump looking exactly like its neighbour. There was scarcely a gap to be seen, so thickly had the clumps grown.

The light was fading rapidly. Something must have happened to Perkin. He wouldn't willingly stay all by himself in the dark, would he? It wasn't as though he came of a dedicated hunting breed, like the Jack Russells. Father had owned a Jack Russell — or been owned by her — in my childhood. She had vanished periodically in pursuit of rats or rabbits.

"Helen dear, see if you can find Twinkle," Father would call. "She ran off into the meadow . . . "

"Why bother? She'll come back," Mother would answer impatiently.

"I'm afraid she might get herself stuck down a rabbit hole, or wander into the road and be run over," Father would say anxiously.

He always felt responsible for the dog and wouldn't rest until he had her safely back again.

I hadn't consciously thought of Twinkle for years. As a child, I had wondered vaguely why Father used to worry so much about her, because she always did turn up again, often mud- or soil-encrusted, but wagging her stump of a tail and greeting Father as if *he* had gone missing.

Perhaps it was the subconscious memory of his anxiety which had kept me from ever wanting a dog of my own. Perhaps, subconsciously, I had realised that I shouldn't be able to withhold my affection and devotion and would be inviting heart-break . . .

"Perkin! Perkin . . . " I was pacing up and down the path, calling despairingly: "Please, please, Perkin, come back to missus! There's a good boy now . . . Perkin . . . "

I knew a sudden, almost physical hunger for the feel of that soft, furry, puppy body in my arms, for the eager tongue, the floppy paws, the white-tipped tail and the lustrous brown eyes welcoming me trustfully and lovingly. Perkin did love and trust me. He couldn't really want to run away from me. He would have come back, panting and prancing, if something hadn't prevented him.

Oh, how could I find him? In the darkness, it would be hopeless. Should I go back to the caravan for my torch? But . . . supposing he came out and I'd gone? Oh, where was Shadrack? He ought to be here to help me. My eyes were blurred. From the salt wind or from unshed tears? I felt like flopping down and howling — but what good would that do to the pup?

I trudged on along the uneven path, splashing in and out of puddles, ears and eyes straining. Was that a whimper? I hadn't come as far as this before. The reeds seemed denser and I could faintly distinguish bulrushes behind them.

"Perkin! Perkin, *come!*" My voice sounded hoarse and despairing. "Good Perkin . . . "

He barked . . . his funny little puppy bark . . . and my heart thudded. He was here somewhere. He had heard me.

"Perkin! Perkin, bark!" I called imperatively. "Where are you?"

He barked again . . . and then I heard a high, thin wail. It sounded so eerily human that a shiver ran down my spine. I'd never heard a sound like that from Perkin before. Was he in a trap? In agony? Traps were illegal now, weren't they? Perhaps poachers still used them.

Fear lent impetus to my tired, flagging limbs. I plunged recklessly into the reeds. They whipped at my face and hair and I had to fight my way through them. Then my feet were embedded in soft, sticky mud and water was oozing into my shoes.

More barks . . . and another thin wail. Oh, why hadn't I a torch? I was among the bulrushes now and they were above my head. I was in a cage. I couldn't get free. I threshed about me wildly — and nearly fell headlong as the rushes thinned and parted. I landed on my hands and knees on wet grass. There was a kind of mound, a grassy bank . . . and a miniature stream, with clumps of osiers, beside it.

Then, oh joy, oh bliss! there was a wet nose against my chin, and muddy paws on my arms.

"Perkin . . . oh, *Perkin* . . . " I gasped, and tried to hug him, but he was held fast, his lead wrapped tightly round a trailing osier branch.

I struggled to free the lead, but it wasn't merely caught round the branch. It was tied to it. Yes, *tied*. Human fingers had secured that knot. Perkin's frantic struggles had obviously tightened it. My numbed and fumbling hands simply couldn't undo it. I could have howled from sheer frustration and rising fury. Who — who could have tied my puppy here, where he might have died wretchedly of starvation and exposure?

In my over-charged emotional state, I was stupidly afraid to unsnap the lead from his collar. I was in terror that he might vanish into the darkness. Later, of course, when I was rational again, I realised that to run away from me again was the very last thing the wet and shivering pup was likely to do. He was trying all he knew to snuggle into my arms . . .

The knot was beyond me. I grabbed the branch. I bent it this way and that, heedless of twig-scratched hands. Eventually, reluctantly, it broke . . . untidily and in long shreds. I had to break the shreds one by one. My endurance and my nerves were as frayed as the osier branch when I heard that wailing cry again.

"Hell!" I said weakly, shuddering, because it hadn't been the wriggling pup who had made that eerie sound. "What on earth — ?"

I was thoroughly ashamed of it, but my first impulse was to gather up Perkin plus the broken branch, and flee. If there was some other animal here, in distress, it was really no concern of mine. It could hardly be another dog. It must be some creature of the wild. Injured? Probably — but what could I do for it? A wounded fox or badger or even an otter would be more than I could hope — or dare — to tackle.

The cry came again. It sounded most horribly, unnervingly human. A vixen, perhaps?

I could, at least, find out, my conscience scolded me. I needn't touch the wailing creature. I could, somehow, mark the spot and go for help, even if the only help that could be offered consisted of a humane killer. I couldn't run away and leave something to suffer . . .

When I had manœuvred myself, the osier branch and Perkin round the osier clump, I perceived dimly that there was quite a stretch of grassy bank before the next clump of osiers. A picnic spot? Just possibly, in the holiday season, I supposed, as I discerned a battered ice-cream container, a sodden cigarette packet, and some indistinguishable scraps of débris strewn at the base of the osiers. People! The careless, unthinking kind would leave sordid traces of their presence virtually anywhere and everywhere. With my innate, incurable distaste for mess and muddle, I had a fierce contempt for people who marred the natural beauty of the shore and countryside with their horrid litter. Bits of eggshell and orange peel and sticky cartons made my stomach heave. In the dim light, I trod on a battered Coke tin and it rolled away down the bank into the stream.

I winced. I wanted desperately to get away from this desolate spot. I longed for the neat orderliness of Shadrack's bungalow; for a hot cup of tea and a hot bath. I hadn't actually been in close contact with grime or soggy litter, but I felt as if I had. The caravan could have been a refuge, but it had been spoilt for me now by cheap perfume and cigarette stubs. Why that cheap, cloying scent should be more repellent than an expensive brand would have been, I couldn't have said. Any perfume would have indicated a female intruder. Was I snob enough to feel that an intrusion by the type of people who dropped cigarette stubs on the floor and used that sickly scent was worse than a similar intrusion

171

by more sophisticated and civilised folk?

There was moisture in my eyes again, blurring my sight. From the salt breeze or from chagrin and self-pity? I fumbled in my pocket for a handkerchief or a face tissue. I couldn't find either. That trivial deprivation added to my discomfort to an absurd degree.

I had found Perkin. I ought to feel immensely relieved; even jubilant. I stooped to run my chilly fingers through his soft fur. I was supremely thankful . . . of course, I was. I was also increasingly uneasy; almost afraid. I had to force myself to walk on across the wet grass to the far clump of osiers.

Silence now, except for the rustle of the reeds and the distant splash of the waves. Perhaps that creature I was so reluctantly looking for was already beyond help? Dared I try to convince myself that any further search would be futile?

Perkin whimpered and pulled on the lead suddenly, so that osier twigs scratched my knuckles as I clung to the broken-off branch.

"Don't! Quietly!" I snapped.

Then I saw what he was straining

towards. It looked like a small bundle of clothes, at the foot of the next osiers . . . but it was moving just perceptibly. Or — was that my imagination?

I swallowed hard. Not another half-drowned puppy! I thought in acute dismay. Perhaps it was a kitten this time. Something alive must be agitating that bundle. Was it a discarded sack? No, it was a shabby anorak. Perkin was nosing the bundle. He jumped back with a frightened yelp as another thin wail rent the air.

Still hanging on to the osier branch tightly, I stooped to investigate. With my free hand — and an acute sense of apprehension — I pulled back the padded nylon, to reveal a crumpled, wizened little face. A monkey? How could there possibly be a monkey here, among the reed-beds? It seemed almost as incredible that a human baby could have been abandoned in such conditions, but human the creature obviously was. A tentative finger on its chin confirmed that surmise.

"Oh, *dear!*" I said weakly and inadequately. "As if I hadn't trouble enough already! Now, what do I do?"

The answer was as self-evident as it was unwelcome. I couldn't leave a tiny baby here while I went for help. I might be unable to find the spot again before the baby died of exposure. It was even more vulnerable than the puppy.

Again, I felt like howling. Why should this have happened to *me*? My father would say that I had been led here . . . to save this baby's life. That could well be true, but why did it have to be my lot to stumble to the rescue? I was filled with a burning rage against the utterly heartless human who had tied my puppy to the osier and left his or her new-born infant to perish miserably. The rage did at least send a warming current through my tired body and galvanise me into movement.

Clumsily, I scooped the bundle up under my right arm, and bent to retrieve the osier branch. Once away from that grassy bank and in among the rushes and reeds, there was barely a glimmering of daylight left.

It was a nightmare journey. The branch and Perkin's lead kept on getting caught up and had to be wrenched free. The baby, tiny though it was, felt like a lump of lead hugged to me. My sodden shoes slipped and slithered. I was panting and gasping, long before I felt the pebbles of the path beneath my feet.

There must obviously have been a track of some kind, leading to that bank above the stream, but I had failed to locate it. I had fought and crashed my way through to firm ground. Sweat was pouring down my face and spine. Perkin was whimpering, but the baby was ominously quiet. I hoped fervently that it hadn't died on me.

Someone had plainly intended that it should die, just as plainly as that brute had intended to drown Perkin and his brothers and sisters. How could one like and trust people when members of the human race were capable of such cold-blooded savagery? Suppose one fell in love with a man, only to discover too late that he possessed that unforgivable streak of cruelty in him?

I could protest: "Oh, not Micky! Not Shadrack — " but how did I know? Father would say that no Christian could ever be cruel or heartless but, somehow, one hesitated to question a newly made friend about his or her personal beliefs. By the time one knew a person really well, it could be too late. Perhaps that was what had befallen the mother of this helpless mite. She might have felt herself betrayed and abandoned by the baby's father. Even so, that was no excuse for just dumping the baby.

I experienced a few more horrible moments when I reached the carpark and couldn't immediately locate the Fiesta. I stumbled across the worn concrete with flying spray and the stiffening breeze stinging my skin and making my eyes water. There was barely a glimmer of light now and the carpark seemed to stretch for acres. Had I blundered past the exit?

Perkin baulked suddenly and then tugged me sideways. I might have guessed that, young though he was, his sense of direction was better than mine. To him, a car evidently stood for home and shelter. He led me right up to the Fiesta.

Thankfully, I forgave him for the anxiety and distress he had inflicted on me earlier. After all, he had had a good reason for rushing off to investigate. He must have followed the baby's mother. Who else would have tied him to that osier?

He might well have been present at the baby's birth, I realised, a minute or two later, as I laid the anorak-wrapped baby on the back seat. By the car's interior light, I saw that the infant was stark naked and hadn't even been bathed yet. It was still breathing — to my profound relief — but its little wrinkled face was an ominous bluish-white.

I unsnapped Perkin's lead at last, and tossed away the osier bough. He needed no urging to scramble into the car. I put him on the front passenger seat and he nuzzled my arm affectionately.

Surely, Shadrack must have returned by now? I thought hopefully, as I started up the engine. I needed the facilities of the bungalow . . . warm water, towels and some kind of wrappings for the baby. Milk, and a bottle, too. There just might be a feeding bottle among the goods stocked by the camp's shop. Such shops carried an extensive range during their short season. If not, Shadrack would have to find a chemist's where the owner lived on the premises.

This weekend seemed to have lasted interminably long, but it was only Sunday evening, I remembered. There wouldn't be any shops open on a Sunday evening in October. Perhaps it would be wiser to contact the nearest hospital, but the baby might die while I was driving around looking for a hospital. I needed a telephone. I needed Shadrack . . .

10

I MUST have been almost light-headed from mental and physical exhaustion. Certainly, I wasn't thinking clearly or, when I found the bungalow dark, deserted and locked, I should have headed for the nearest call-box.

Instead, leaving Perkin and the baby shut in the car, I groped my way towards the camp's shop, calling: "Shadrack! Shadrack, where are you?"

Did I hope to find him in the shop, checking over the stock? Or did I intend to break into it in search of a baby's bottle? My head was spinning and my knees threatened to buckle under me. The chilly breeze was sending shivers down my sweating back. I hadn't been designed for this kind of situation. I wasn't nearly tough enough or resourceful enough. All that obsessed me was my burning need of Shadrack.

"A man to lean on!" my mother might have pronounced in mild scorn. "You're not as self-sufficient as you imagine, Helen. In any crisis, you'll always look for a man's support."

"Shadrack! *Shadrack!*" I bleated, despair seeping into me again. I nearly jumped out of my clammy skin when a groan answered me.

"What is it? Who's there?" I quavered — and heard another groan. "Shadrack — "

"Help!"

Help, indeed? That was what I needed, wasn't it?

"Who? Where?" I tried to scoop up my oozing courage. "Is — is someone hurt?"

"Helen? Helen, is that you?"

The voice was husky, but unmistakably Shadrack's.

"Yes! Yes, I'm here. Where are you?"

Instinctively, I was heading for the darkness between two rows of caravans, from which his voice seemed to proceed. I had to find him . . .

"Ooh!" I gasped — as I cannoned into something solid, and choked back a scream as a hand clawed at my legs.

"Here! Steady! Why in heaven's name didn't you bring a torch?" Shadrack's

180

voice sounded aggrieved as well as husky. "That hurt — "

"Sorry! My torch is in the caravan. I — What's the matter? What are you doing here? Are you sitting on the ground? Why?"

"Because some ruffian knocked me out and trussed me up like an oven-ready chicken," he grunted. "I'd only just surfaced and was trying to get up when I heard your call. Oh, hell! My head . . . "

"Oh, never mind your head! You're here," I said in fervent relief. "You're tied up? Haven't you a knife? I thought men always carried pocket knives."

"Perhaps you'll be kind enough to tell me how I extract a knife from my pocket when my hands are secured behind my back?" he demanded ironically.

"You're recovering. You're all right," I said thankfully. "Keep still and I'll find the knife . . . "

I discovered by touch, not sight, that he was sprawled out on his face. I located the pocket knife eventually and set to work to hack through the cord — it felt like clothes line — which was binding his wrists. It was no easy task in the darkness and I was terrified of cutting into one of his veins.

"Thanks, Helen!" he said gruffly as the last strands parted. "Better give me the knife . . . "

He tried to take it from me but his hands were numbed and he dropped it. I had to fumble around for it, while he complained again of my lack of foresight in omitting to bring a torch.

"Oh, stop grizzling!" I said crossly. "I dare say I should have put my torch in your car but how was I to guess that I'd need it? If you'd been around when I got back, I shouldn't have gone down to the beach and been caught out in the darkness. It was very silly of you to let someone knock you over the head."

"Silly? Is that all the sympathy you can offer a wounded hero?"

"You're no hero — and you're not badly hurt or you wouldn't be sarcastic," I retorted, retrieving the knife by stabbing a finger on the open blade. "Ouch! I've found it . . . and I've cut my finger."

"That'll learn you!" he said darkly. "You're no heroine. Heroines always come supplied with torches and scissors."

"And baby's bottles and nappies! You're not the only one who's had a grim time, let me assure you! Someone broke into my caravan and stole the only valuable object in it. Then, I lost Perkin in that horrible reed-bed and found a new-born baby."

"Baby? What the heck are you burbling about? What kind of baby?"

"A human baby. That's why I was looking for you."

"For me? I don't own any babies."

"Are you sure of that? Anyway, you've the keys to the bungalow, and if the baby isn't bathed and warmed and fed, it'll die," I said urgently. "There now! Try to move your feet . . . "

He groaned but I seized him by his shoulders and heaved him into a sitting position.

"Come on now! You can stand up if you try," I admonished him.

"Have a heart, woman! Pins and needles," he said ruefully. "Agonising. Like thawing out after frostbite."

"Hard luck! Well, if you want to stay here, groaning, give me the keys."

"Oh, Helen, my love! You can't leave me helpless here to perish of exposure," he protested reproachfully, and I sensed that he wasn't altogether joking. He really was feeling shaky. "Besides, I can't let you wander around here alone among lurking thugs . . . "

"I expect the thugs have cleared out . . . " but uneasiness stirred in me again.

Shadrack was in no condition to defend himself — or me — and I had left the Fiesta unlocked.

"Come on!" I urged him again. "Let's get to the bungalow."

"Give me a hand up, then!"

He staggered and leaned heavily on me. I could feel that this was an endurance test for him, as we moved at a snail's pace up the path between the caravans.

"Who knocked you out? And why?" I asked, to distract his attention from his aches and pains.

"My pseudo-cousin, I fancy. A tough looking character with a beard. I had only a fleeting glimpse of him."

"How did you come across him?"

"I told you I intended to investigate.

I heard voices — raised and angry. There seemed, from the sounds that reached me, to be a furious row in progress between two females. One was screeching: 'I'll kill you! I'll never give him up . . . never . . . never!' and the man was shouting to them both to 'cool it', when I arrived on the scene." He put one hand to his head, wryly. "I'd got as far as demanding: 'What the heck's going on here?' when the bearded chap seized an oar and swung at me. I tried to dodge it, but it caught me across the back of my head. Ouch!"

"He might have killed you. Oh, Shadrack! . . . "

"Would you have cared? Would you, Helen?" he demanded.

"Of course. Anyone would. What a silly question!"

"I wasn't asking about 'anyone'. I was asking about you. Do I matter at all?"

"Very much. Do you have the keys of the shop on you? There might be a baby's bottle among the stock . . . "

"A baby's bottle?" he repeated dazedly.

"I told you. Weren't you listening? I found a baby and it needs to be fed."

"Sorry! I'm still a bit confused. Did you say you had a baby?"

"I said I'd found a baby," I repeated impatiently. "Where are those keys? No. I must get a torch first. I suppose you've a torch indoors somewhere?"

"There's one in my car. In the boot."

"Heavens! Why didn't I think to look there? I am an idiot . . . "

"As a matter of fact, the light's still working in the shop. I haven't had a chance to check the stock yet, so the electricity hasn't been disconnected."

"Oh, joy! There should be some baby's things . . . "

"Probably, but I can't imagine why you want a baby. Isn't the pup enough for you?" he asked blankly.

"I don't want a baby! I found a baby . . . and I can't just let it die, can I?" I said reasonably. "The keys, Shadrack . . . "

Caravan holidays were popular with family parties, I knew, and caravan camps derived quite a nice addition to their incomes from their takings at the camp shops. Most shops, like the traditional village Post Office-cum-Stores, carried

186

a surprisingly comprehensive range of goods. The Heatherview Shop was bigger and better laid out than most. No untidy jumble of stuff here. One end, dominated by an enormous deep freeze, and a glass fronted counter over a refrigerated compartment was equipped to deal with food and drinks, with shelves for tinned and packaged foods. To one side, there were holiday requirements — sparse now, with just a few swim-suits, gym shoes, buckets, spades, and suntan lotions left.

Babies had a corner to themselves; a large, open-fronted cupboard with a few remaining tins of baby foods, plus some lotions and powders, and disposable nappies.

"Everything we need, bar a bottle," I said disappointedly. "Nappies, baby oil . . . and . . . yes, here's a bottle. Just one. Tucked away behind the nappies. We're in luck, Shadrack!"

"Are we? I really don't think . . . " He was leaning against the door. By the overhead strip lighting, he looked pale and haggard. "You're in a fearful mess. Did you know? You've a scratch right across your throat and your hands are bleeding. They're grimy, too. You need to wash them thoroughly and put antiseptic on those scratches."

"Naturally, I'm in a mess — from what I've been through. You don't look so hot, let me tell you," I retorted tartly. "Come on — and let's hope there's some hot water."

"The immersion heater is on, so there should be."

"That's fine!"

If I had never before appreciated the blessing of a steady flow of hot water, I was truly thankful for it this evening. I bathed the baby, the puppy, and myself, in that order. I fed the baby and the puppy and tucked them up warmly before I got into a steaming hot bath. Both were sleeping peacefully when I emerged. I couldn't bring myself to don those stained, soaked and mud-encrusted slacks again. I fastened a capacious bath towel around my waist, as an improvised skirt. My shirt and sweater had fortunately been protected by my rain-coat.

Shadrack had made coffee. When he had poured out a fragrant cupful for me, he said abruptly: "I've rung the police."

"The police? Oh, *why*?" I asked in involuntary dismay.

"My dear girl, be reasonable! It's all very well to rescue and adopt a half-drowned puppy. You can't simply appropriate a human baby in the same way," he pointed out. "Besides, the mother must need help."

"The mother? Who cares about *her*? Anyone who can abandon a helpless, new-born baby — " I began indignantly, but he cut me short with: "Must be in an abnormal condition mentally, and certainly in need of skilled attention."

"Oh! I hadn't thought of that. I'm afraid I haven't been thinking clearly," I admitted in sudden compunction. "I was so tensed up . . . about losing Perkin . . . and frightened, too, among those seemingly interminable reeds."

"Tell me," he said, in a gentler tone.

He had switched on an electric fire, so the room felt pleasantly warm. The warmth was very welcome. Even after the hot bath, my limbs still felt sore and aching, though the scratches had stopped bleeding.

Shadrack was not a charmer, but he

was a comforting kind of character. He had a nice sense of proportion and of priorities. He had refrained from catechising me until I could sink back and relax. Perkin was emerging from the rug in which I had wrapped him. He shook himself and then trotted across to me and hauled himself up on to my lap. I hugged him contentedly. I had never guessed that an unwanted pup could become of importance to me; become part of my life. It would be a long time, if ever, before I ceased to be haunted by the terror and desolation I had experienced tonight.

"You're shivering again," Shadrack said concernedly. "I'll get you a blanket."

"Shuddering, not shivering," I amended, but I was glad of the fleecy blanket which he fetched and wrapped round me. "I don't remember that I'd ever been really frightened before."

As I sipped the hot coffee, which he had laced with brandy, I managed to give him a fairly coherent account of my adventures. He was properly sympathetic but obviously mystified.

"Why did you go down to the shore just as the light was fading?" he inquired.

"You could have let the pup run around in the camp."

"I suppose I was hunting for you," I felt compelled to admit. "I imagined that you had gone down there to watch the evening flights. The birds seemed to be flying in to roost."

"I see! That was nice of you." He smiled in an absurdly gratified fashion. "You wanted to find me? So — you hadn't kissed and made up with that Micky fellow?"

"Oh, no! I couldn't. I saw that almost at once. I felt rather badly about it, because he had bought a diamond engagement ring for me."

"Had he now? Genuine?"

"Certainly. A very fine ring," I answered with dignity. Then, honesty made me add: "Not brand-new, though. And he simply couldn't see that I would have preferred an inexpensive garnet or amethyst ring, bought specially for me, to a costly diamond ring acquired secondhand as an investment."

"You would? That's interesting. Unusual, wouldn't you say?"

"I've no idea. I don't care for

diamonds, anyway. They have that hard glitter and they seem to me to have shrill voices, proclaiming 'money'. The coloured stones have a much gentler beauty."

"Like yourself," he nodded. "Yes. You're quite right. Diamonds are not you. So you gave the man his ring back? Splendid!"

"I couldn't. It has vanished. Micky is going to be terribly vexed about that," I said with foreboding. "It was scarcely my fault, though. I thought I was giving him a break by hiding it. After all, it could have been Millicent Forrester's."

That provoked further questions from Shadrack and I was obliged to admit to my half-formed suspicions of Micky. I hastened to add that Micky himself had effectively dispelled them. Shadrack remained sceptical. It was too much of a coincidence to swallow, that a second car, identical with mine, could have been involved, he reasoned.

"I know," I said wearily. "But . . . I believe Micky."

"Then, you must still care about him."

Did I? To some extent, certainly, but

not in the way Shadrack was implying.

Before I could evolve a suitable answer, the doorbell sounded an imperative summons.

"That must be the police," Shadrack surmised.

"Oh dear! What am I to tell them?" I asked anxiously.

"Just the plain truth. What else?"

"If I knew it, I dare say I would, but what is the truth?"

"Stick to the facts and leave the police to sort them out." Shadrack gave me an odd, penetrating glance as he heaved himself out of his armchair in response to a second, prolonged ring.

"If your conscience is clear, why are you looking so worried?"

"*You* obviously don't believe my story, so why should the police?" I countered. "Perhaps you don't even believe that I found this baby?"

"Oh, yes! I believe that. You're just the kind of girl who would make such a bizarre discovery," he answered, lips quirking into a half smile.

Whether that was a criticism or a compliment, I couldn't guess.

11

'THE police' turned out to be a lanky young constable, and a plump but trimly uniformed W.P.C. Neither of them appeared to know what to make of me or my story.

The W.P.C., who looked to be in her early thirties, kept on glancing speculatively from me to Shadrack and back again, as if she suspected us of complicity in some dark plot to rid ourselves of the infant.

"It's not mine," I repeated in exasperation, "and I certainly don't want it, but I couldn't leave it there to die, could I?"

"It?" the W.P.C. echoed, with a lift of her neatly plucked eyebrows. "Boy or girl?"

"A girl, actually, but it looks like an 'it', don't you think? Rather like a wizened monkey, but quite normal, as far as I can see. It — she fed from the bottle readily enough."

The lanky P.C., who to my way of thinking would have been improved by a hair-cut, was irritatingly earnest and methodical. He insisted on writing down my "full name, age, address, and occupation", and then demanded similar particulars from Shadrack.

"This is all beside the point," Shadrack told him impatiently. "I contacted you in order that you might lay on a search for the baby's mother. She may well be in a parlous condition."

"The baby's mother?" the P.C. repeated, ball point pen poised. "Her name would be — ?"

"How would I know? She could be anyone . . . local or a visitor," Shadrack retorted. "It's possible that she was occupying one of the caravans illegally. She could have been one of the two females I heard abusing one another . . . "

To have retailed that scrap of information was plainly an error in judgment. The young P.C. seized upon it avidly and questioned Shadrack in minute detail. He brightened visibly when Shadrack was obliged to explain why he hadn't had a glimpse of either contestant.

"Struck on the back of the head with an oar," he observed, with an air of relish. "assaulted by an unknown intruder. Trespass with intent. Breaking and entering. Grievous bodily harm . . . "

"Oh, call it what you please, but get cracking!" Shadrack snapped. "That wretched young woman may be in a state of collapse, somewhere down on the shore. And the child should be taken to hospital."

It wasn't as simple as that; at least not to our two constables. Searches for missing persons were only initiated after families or friends had reported them missing, we were informed. Babies were only admitted to hospital at the request of the doctor with whom they or their parents were registered under the National Health . . .

"Red tape! Ridiculous," Shadrack said indignantly.

On the other hand, inquiries as to the whereabouts of the bearded intruder could be undertaken immediately.

"A full description would help."

I was able to furnish that and did so, a little puzzled by Shadrack's obvious exasperation. He didn't appear to care whether the man who had knocked him out was 'apprehended' by our lanky P.C. or not. His concern was for the baby's mother. Why? Had he recognised her voice? Could she have been a former girl friend of his?

After the callous way in which she had tied Perkin to that osier and abandoned him and her baby, that female wasn't deserving of any consideration, I thought censoriously. The baby, who was merely an innocent victim, did rate some skilled care and attention. She should be seen by a doctor and transferred to a children's ward.

"Can't you take the baby with you and drop her off at the nearest hospital?" I appealed to the W.P.C. "Really, I can't be responsible for her."

Her reply made it plain that she considered I had assumed the responsibility by removing the baby. Had I left the child in the clearing and summoned the police, they would have taken over, as in duty bound.

"That's mere quibbling!" I was becoming exasperated now. "Would you have expected me to leave the poor mite there? She might have been dead by the time you'd arrived on the scene. I might not have been able to find the right place again, anyway. Use your common-sense, please!"

At that, the plump policewoman got to her feet, and announced stiffly that she would contact 'headquarters', make her report and 'elicit instructions'.

"Elicit some action, for heaven's sake!" Shadrack exploded. "D'you want to use this telephone?"

She declined the offer. They had their own means of communication in their patrol car, she explained, and marched out, very erect and heavy-footed.

The lanky P.C. unbent enough to give me a grin and remark that: "Carter doesn't go for babies. You won't get her to take this one off your hands, and we've no facilities for housing kids or stray dogs at the Station. Looks like you're stuck with 'em both."

"Both? Oh, but the puppy is mine! I adopted him over a week ago," I said, hugging Perkin closer.

It would be typical of this precious pair to impound the puppy and leave me with the baby, I reflected crossly and probably unfairly. Where were the brisk, helpful policemen of the advertisements? I had been right, all along, to refrain from contact with the police. Perhaps Shadrack would admit that now. I glanced at him, but he was still nattering on about the baby's mother, and her physical, mental and emotional condition.

"You're quite certain that you can't put a name to her?" the P.C. asked in a sceptical tone. "Not even to make a guess?"

So . . . he was thinking what I was trying hard not to think? Why should Shadrack be het up about a complete stranger's possible sufferings?

Shadrack shook his head impatiently and the P.C. said meaningly: "Odd that you were attacked without any cause. There wasn't any jealousy — any unpleasantness — over a girl friend?"

"Certainly not!" Shadrack retorted emphatically.

This time, he glanced at me as if

for sympathy. I looked back at him woodenly. He had insisted on calling in 'the police'. It was up to him to cope with them. To some extent, I could read the young P.C.'s mind. There might be kudos and possible promotion in catching a man who could be charged with causing grievous bodily harm. To track down the distraught mother who had abandoned her baby was unlikely to lead to any court proceedings.

"An unprovoked assault," he persisted. "According to your statement, Mr Heston, it was unprovoked?"

"The fellow was trespassing," Shadrack said shortly. "And he had obtained £50 from Miss Melville under false pretences."

I could almost see the young P.C.'s rather prominent ears, only partially concealed by his long limp hair, pricking themselves up at that additional information.

"False pretences?" he echoed eagerly.

"He made me believe that he was in a position to let me rent a caravan here for a week," I explained reluctantly.

That evoked more questions, of course, irritating and time wasting. The P.C. was like a terrier with a bone; determined to gnaw the last vestige of meat from it.

I was momentarily glad when the plump W.P.C. Carter returned . . . until I perceived the pleased glitter in her round china-blue eyes, and the smirk with which she inquired: "You are Miss Helen Melville, of High Rise, Malbury, near Plymouth, Devon?"

"I'm Helen Melville, and I did stay at High Rise, Malbury, for a time," I answered cautiously. "Why?"

"You're wanted for questioning in connection with the disappearance of some jewellery," she informed me, savouring the words as if they tasted sweetly. "If you'll kindly accompany us to the Station, the Superintendent will take your statement."

"Accompany you? I can't," I said flatly, pulling the blanket more closely round me. "I haven't anything to wear."

The china-blue eyes focused on my bath-towel and blanket with avidity.

"Draw what conclusions you please," I told their owner tartly. "The unromantic fact is that I've been in the reed-beds, and emerged soaked and mud-stained.

I've just had a hot bath and my slacks are still saturated. I can't go anywhere like this. Besides, I've no information to give you."

"That's for the Superintendent to decide," W.P.C. Carter said primly. "We must request you to accompany us."

"Request away! You can't compel me to go with you. Not unless you've a warrant for my arrest," I said crossly.

"Miss Melville has not visited Malbury since she left there, over a week ago," Shadrack interposed. "She doesn't know anything about this alleged robbery."

"Alleged?" she echoed sharply.

"No signs of breaking and entering, from the account in the newspapers. Sounds a fishy affair to me," Shadrack retorted. "Most likely one of those insurance frauds."

"Miss Melville's car was seen in the immediate vicinity yesterday."

"I very much doubt that," I demurred.

"In any event, Miss Melville was not using her car. She had lent it to a friend," Shadrack added, firmly. "You have no grounds at all for badgering her."

He shouldn't have said that, I thought

unhappily. Now, their air of frank scepticism even more in evidence, the constables insisted on being given the name and address of the 'friend'. When, reluctantly, I mentioned the Down to Earth Community Centre, they snapped at it like trout swallowing a fly.

"Had our eye on that place for months past," W.P.C. Carter proclaimed. "There have been complaints . . . " She pursed up her full lips primly. "From more than one source. You have friends there, Miss Melville."

"One friend."

"And he borrowed the car? A yellow Peugeot, registration number BTT 9990?" she repeated.

"Yes. But . . . not to visit Malbury. He was in Dorchester."

"That's his story?" She gave me a feline smile. "We're to bring the car to the Station, with your permission, of course, Miss Melville."

"Or without it?" I hazarded. "Take her and give her the once over with my blessing — if you can find her. I haven't seen her since this morning."

That started them off again. Shadrack

and I exchanged glances which were the equivalent of heartfelt groans. My glance held an additional flavour of reproach. He had brought this tiresome and seemingly interminable ordeal upon us. He should have foreseen that I was hopelessly enmeshed. Even to unprejudiced, friendly ears my story must have sounded improbable, if not actually 'fishy'. Nothing that had happened to me since I had left Malbury had been simple and straightforward.

"Oh, for heaven's sake!" Shadrack exploded at last. "We've told you all we know. Get cracking and find this baby's mother — and Miss Melville's car. You're merely wasting time here."

Whether they would have gone then or not, I couldn't guess. Luckily, as I realised later, at that juncture the baby woke up and rent the air with piercing cries.

"It's hungry — or wet. Both, probably." I fixed W.P.C. Carter with a steady gaze. "Would you care to change and feed it? I'm afraid I'm rather exhausted. Indeed, I'm beginning to feel quite faint . . . "

"And no wonder, after all you've been

through!" Shadrack was swift to seize his cue. "How long is it since you had any solid food?"

"Ages," I answered mournfully. "I expect it's part of the policewoman's training to learn how to cope with babies and child-birth. Do you get badges, like the Girl Guides', for proficiency in this and that?"

The lanky P.C. grinned, but his colleague's expression was stony as she said hurriedly that it was time they reported back to 'the Station'.

"So one would imagine. Not exactly 'The Sweeney', are you?" Shadrack said pointedly. "Couldn't you drop the baby off at a hospital on your way?"

That had the desired effect of hastening their departure. Shadrack was frowning as he closed and locked the door after them.

"It's too bad! Why should you have to look after this infant? You're worn out already," he said wrathfully. "Look, you'd better put on my dressing-gown, while I go along to the caravan and collect your things."

"Oh, don't bother!"

"I'd better. You'd be lost in my pyjamas and I don't have a spare toothbrush."

"But — "

"No 'buts'. You're staying here tonight. There is a guest-room. I'm not letting you sleep in that isolated caravan alone," he said decisively. "That thug may still be on the prowl . . . "

"I didn't guess that you were one of those masterful men," I said, heaving myself up and retrieving the whimpering baby.

"Oddly enough, neither did I," he retorted whimsically. "Mostly, I've tried to keep from becoming involved, emotionally."

"Have you? I think I wanted to be, but somehow I never was," I said reflectively.

"Until now?"

"I didn't say that."

I turned my back on him and busied myself, changing the baby's soaking nappy. When I'd finished, Shadrack was beside me, holding his dressing-gown out to me. It was much too long, but at least it was preferable to the clutched blanket and clammy towel.

"What number's your caravan?" he asked purposefully.

I supposed I wasn't really an independent type. Had I been, I should have insisted on returning to the caravan for the night. I wouldn't admit that I was nervous. It seemed highly improbable that the marauder would visit the caravan again. If he had still been skulking around, wouldn't the arrival of the police car have put him to flight?

I would be safe enough in the caravan, but it would undeniably be cheerless there. Shadrack's guest-room and Shadrack's presence, within call, appeared much more inviting.

"You'll stay here . . . " he said — and it sounded more like an appeal than a command. "Please, Helen!"

He wasn't naturally the kind of man who would push a girl around or walk over her, I thought in relief. It was simply that for some reason or other, he felt protective over me.

"Thank you," I answered demurely. "It'll certainly be warmer here for the baby."

He made a displeased sound at that,

which I ignored. I wasn't going to admit to any form of weakness for him. At least, not yet. Not until I knew more about him, and had discovered why he was so deeply concerned about the baby's mother.

12

"IF we both go, the police may get it into their thick heads that we've bolted," Shadrack said meditatively. "It would be unpleasant to have a hue and cry after us."

"Very!" I agreed. "I can't see what we can hope to gain from tackling Millicent Forrester."

"We can ascertain what game she's playing — if any. I've had quite a lot of experience in interrogating doubtful characters," he explained modestly. "People will imagine that they can trick their accountants. So foolish of them. We're far better versed in every kind of fiddle than most Inland Revenue officials. To extract the true facts from a raw amateur like your Mrs Forrester should be kindergarten stuff."

His eyes were gleaming behind his glasses as he turned from the stove to set a plate bearing a delicious-looking tomato omelette in front of me. I shouldn't, I realised, care to have Shadrack on my trail if I had a guilty conscience. He would evince the patience and persistence of a bloodhound.

"I can't see why you think she is up to some kind of game," I demurred.

"Because I find the whole story implausible. It's all too slick and convenient. No doors forced. No windows smashed. Nobody assaulted or even bound and gagged," he elucidated. "The thief waits until the house is empty, then parks your car where it'll be sure to catch the eye of passers-by, if not of a Traffic Warden, lets him or herself in with a latchkey, collects the jewellery, and calmly drives away again, unaccosted? Is that credible?"

"Not about the car," I conceded. "If Micky swears he wasn't in Malbury, I believe him. I'm certain he wouldn't have been stupid enough to park on double lines. That bit doesn't ring true. Samantha must have been embroidering there."

"And where else? That young woman is crying out to be investigated. Either she is being deliberately malicious, or else she's throwing up a smoke screen to conceal her own actions."

"You could be right, I suppose, but you wouldn't get anything out of her. She is one of those pretty, lively, madly seductive creatures who can make rings round the average man."

"Ah, but I'm not the average man! I'm Shadrack Heston," he retorted, with quiet pride. "Charmers leave me frozen. It takes something like the natural, unstudied warmth of your smile to thaw me."

"Oh?" I glanced at him, uncertain whether he was trying to make me rise or not, but he was pouring out coffee with the calm concentration he seemed to bring to everything he undertook. "Shadrack — "

"In the circumstances, it would be advisable for you to stay here," he went on firmly. "You could keep the door locked, but you should be perfectly safe in daylight, and I'll be back before dark."

I was in a quandary. I most certainly did not want to traipse back to Malbury, to face Millicent Forrester or Samantha Tiggs. Even though they had no grounds for their suspicions of me, those suspicions were hurtful. Moreover, I had the baby and Perkin to consider. One didn't take a new-born baby jaunting around in a car all day if it could possibly be avoided — and for the time being I seemed to be responsible for this unfortunate baby's welfare. Perkin wouldn't relish such a long trip, either.

On the other hand, I was singularly loth to be left here without Shadrack. It was odd how his presence inspired confidence. I had slept peacefully last night, except for having to get up once to minister to a screaming baby. I had felt entirely safe, knowing that he was within call.

"Particulars, please." Shadrack had produced a neat, leather-bound notebook and opened it beside his plate. Forking up pieces of omelette left-handedly, he held a pencil poised in his right hand. "Millicent Forrester, High Rise . . . "

"Wood Lane, Malbury," I said automatically.

"And Samantha Tiggs? She works at the White Frog?"

"Yes. What a good memory you have!"

"Her home address?"

I gave it to him, but I protested when he asked for Sydney Fane's.

"I've no idea where Sydney lives — and why would you interview him, anyway?"

"He could be involved. No matter. Samantha will know where to find him, if he's her boy-friend," Shadrack said confidently. "The household at High Rise?"

"Mrs Forrester, the three children, and Cook. Mrs Tiggs comes in daily, except at weekends."

"You had three children on your hands?"

"Caroline goes to day school, so I had her only in the evenings and at weekends. She's the spoilt, tiresome one. Diana, who's not quite five, and Sara, who's three and a half, are dear little girls."

"As young as that, are they?"

"Yes, but Diana's very bright. She'll be starting school after Christmas. It was just a temporary job," I explained. "Mrs Forrester thinks she'll be able to cope with Sara and the new baby, when it arrives, if Diana and Caroline are both at school. Their father will be at home again then, and I was told that he was very good in helping with the family. He's really fond of children. Millicent Forrester isn't."

"Don't you find it a wrench to care for children and then be obliged to leave them?"

"It is, of course, although I do try not to become too deeply involved. Diana and Sara both howled when I left, and that was rather upsetting, especially as their tears exasperated their mother and she slapped them," I said regretfully. "I hope she has another Nanny for them by now, or they'll be having a grim time, poor little things. Millicent Forrester hasn't much patience. She fancies herself as an intellectual and sees her marriage as a trap."

"For some girls, I suppose it is. Surely, not for you, Helen? Wouldn't you prefer to be looking after your own children rather than some other woman's?"

"In theory, yes, but it would depend on their father, in actual fact," I answered guardedly. "I wouldn't enjoy being in Mrs Forrester's position, with a husband who lives abroad for weeks at a time."

"You would rather have a husband who worked regular hours and came home every night?"

Probably. I don't know. I'm not good with men."

"Do you aspire to be? Wouldn't one man be enough for you?" he asked, with a quirk of his brows.

"Of course."

I bent down to pat Perkin, who was nosing my ankles affectionately. I hoped I wasn't flushing. Men and marriage were not subjects which I could discuss freely and without embarrassment. I was wretchedly self-conscious about my failure to achieve a satisfactory and lasting romance. There was obviously some fatal flaw in me which, no doubt, Shadrack would discover before long.

He might, of course, be put off by Mrs Forrester's account of my 'brutality' to her precious Caroline. I had already paid dearly for that momentary loss of temper. If Shadrack were to accept Mrs Forrester's version, he would certainly revise his opinion of me.

I sighed involuntarily, and he said:

"Cheer up, love! I shan't be away longer than necessary."

"If you imagine — " I began, and looked up to see that he was smiling.

"Wasn't that sigh for me? How disappointing! I was looking forward to being welcomed home tonight."

"You will be, if I'm still here."

"If? Is there an 'if' about it?"

"I could be arrested, I suppose."

"Scarcely. There's no solid evidence against you, and I intend to disprove the apparent evidence against your car," he assured me. "Have a nice, restful day, and don't worry."

So easy for a man to say "Don't worry!" I thought rebelliously, when Shadrack had gone. Men seemed to believe that they could shoulder or solve every problem that burdened a woman. They took their own anxieties seriously enough. Shadrack had been really worked up last night about the baby's mother. Odd that he hadn't referred to her this morning. Did he plan to institute his own search for her, before he drove off to Malbury? Perhaps he had an inkling of where she might be found?

The bungalow seemed unnaturally quiet and empty after Shadrack's departure. I made my bed and washed up the breakfast dishes. He had already made his bed and his bedroom was scrupulously tidy, a peep round his bedroom door told me. I liked people to be orderly, but I was vaguely disappointed that there didn't appear to be anything I could contribute towards his comfort.

Time threatened to hang heavily on my hands. Without a car, I was stranded. I couldn't even take Perkin for a walk, unless I carried the baby with us, and it would be awkward to manage Perkin's lead with a baby in my arms.

Yet, with the perversity of human nature, I wasn't at all pleased when I heard a car's engine in the drive, followed by a ring at the door. Perkin began to bark and the baby began to wail. My first impulse was not to answer the bell but, if it was the police on the doorstep, they were unlikely to go meekly away.

From where I was, in the kitchenette, the doorstep wasn't visible, but, if I crossed to the sitting-room window to look out, I must inevitably be seen. The doorbell rang again and the baby's voice rose with Perkin's. Her funny, wrinkled little face was turning crimson.

Resignedly, I lifted her from the settee and cradled her in my arms, reflecting not for the first time, that I infinitely preferred small children, however tiresome, to new-born babies. One could talk to children and, to some extent, reason with them. Babies were laws unto themselves.

"Hush now! Hush," I admonished the squalling little object. "Quiet, Perkin! Quiet . . . "

I unlocked the door and opened it a fraction; not wide enough to allow Perkin to bound out on his own. Was I relieved or dismayed to see not the dark blue uniforms of the police but Micky's sleek head and elegant jacket and slacks?

"So — this is where you're hiding yourself? I thought you said you'd hired a caravan?" he hailed me.

"I had, but someone ransacked it and — oh, leave, Perkin!" Awkwardly, I stooped to catch Perkin's collar and hold him back from his patent determination to chew one of Micky's shoe laces. "Do you want to come in, Micky?"

"Naturally."

"Then, shut the door after you. I don't want the puppy to get out. I had a fearful hunt for him last night," I said breathlessly, backing away from the door and dragging Perkin with me. "Oh, hush up, baby, do!"

"So — Lettice was right after all?" Micky exclaimed, on a reproachful note. "You have had a baby."

"Oh, don't be an idiot! Of course I haven't."

"Then, where did that one come from, may I ask?"

"You can ask — and I wish I had the answer. I've no idea," I said shortly. "Sit down, do, and then perhaps Perkin will let your shoes alone!"

I flopped down on the settee and rocked the squalling infant until her piercing cries subsided. Micky seated himself in an armchair, shooing Perkin away with both hands.

"D'you mean that you've landed another job? Already?" Micky demanded sceptically.

"No. I haven't."

"Then whose baby is that?"

"I don't know. I found her. Last night, when I was hunting for Perkin."

Perhaps I didn't tell it very fluently or convincingly, because I was flustered and at a disadvantage, but did Micky have to eye me with such dour suspicion as I gave him my account of last evening's events?

"It all sounds a bit fishy," he commented, when I paused to draw breath. "I'd much rather you were frank with me. Then I should know where I stand."

"Stand where you please, but for any sake use your intelligence! Did I ever look as if I were pregnant?" I demanded in exasperation.

"No. You didn't. That's what foxed me. That and your apparently naive, open nature." He gazed at me almost sorrowfully. "I really was all for you, Curly. You had me tied up in knots."

"But — you've contrived to free yourself?" I taxed him. "Oh dear! I'll have to change this infant again."

He watched in glum silence while I performed the necessary operation. The wails ceased abruptly. The mite actually made chuckling sounds at me. This was one tough baby, I decided thankfully. She was quite determined to survive. She chuckled, and then promptly went off to sleep again.

"A real little mother," Micky said, on a jaundiced note.

"I'm not a mother, but I did train as a child's nurse." I settled the baby back on the settee and braced myself. "Why did you come here, Micky? Simply to check up on me?"

He shook his head.

"I did some serious thinking after you'd left me. I realised that you weren't intending to change your mind and take me on for keeps. It was a blow — no use pretending it wasn't — but I'm not one to weep over spilt milk. I've learnt how and when to cut my losses."

"No," I agreed. "You wouldn't weep. You'd sell the spilt milk at a cut rate to the nearest cat owner."

A slight frown was his only acknowledgment of that sally.

"So — I said to myself that I might as well accept Lord Porterhaven's commission," he went on doggedly. "I've arranged deals for his lordship from time to time, and he'd turned to me in desperation a month ago. Only then I was hard after you."

"Sorry! I'm not with you. How did I hinder you from accepting a commission?" I asked blankly.

Micky, for once, looked self-conscious.

"Well, you see, he was worried sick about his precious daughter. He wanted me to rescue her."

"Rescue her? From what?"

"From the commune. From Foxy and Hal. He promised to make it very much worth my while — and it would be, I don't doubt. He hasn't any other kids. No son and heir. Lettice is his one and only chick."

"Lettice?" I echoed weakly. "Lettice?"

"She's not a bad kid," he said defensively, as he had told me once before. "I can handle her."

"Yes. I expect you can. You shouldn't have any difficulty in cutting out Foxy and Hal," I said in all sincerity. "Is that what you came over here to tell me?"

"Partly. And — to collect the ring. As you haven't any use for it — " He was gazing round the room appraisingly. "Quite a cosy little nest you've found for yourself here. Where's the cock bird?"

"Oh, Micky, don't! There's no need for that resentful tone. This bungalow belongs to a Mr Westcott, the owner of the Heatherview Caravan Camp. Out of season, he lets his nephew use it at weekends. For bird watching."

"Bird watching? Is that what you call it?" He gave a mirthless, un-Micky-like laugh, and I realised again with compunction that I had hurt him. "Can't the fellow find his own birds? Did he have to net mine?"

"He didn't. I'd never even seen him till yesterday morning. It wasn't he who let the caravan to me. He just took pity on me last night, because I was in such a mess and landed with this baby . . . "

It was no use, I thought unhappily. Micky didn't believe me. Perhaps he didn't want to believe me. If he could be sure that I wasn't the girl he had imagined me to be, he would feel himself amply justified in abandoning his pursuit and accepting his lordship's commission. Lettice — and Micky? To visualise that combination did give me a pang, but what right had I to query Micky's future actions? I had dissociated myself from him when I had fled from the commune.

"Somebody had ransacked the caravan, probably while I was with you, yesterday. It was upsetting," I began again. "I was thankful to take refuge here."

"Oh, well, it's no business of mine! Just give me the ring and I'll leave you to it," Micky said with a would-be jaunty air.

"Micky, I can't! I'm terribly sorry. Whoever ransacked my things took your ring. I had hidden it in my sponge-bag. I was sure it would be safe there."

"You've lost it? Heavens, girl! That ring cost me a hundred smackers."

"So you told me. It's most unfortunate."

"Unfortunate! That's an understatement for you! Who pinched it? That fellow you've shacked up with here?"

"Certainly not! And I haven't . . . "

Whether I could have convinced him or not, I had no idea. Our exchange was interrupted abruptly by puppy barks from Perkin, followed by a tapping on the window.

I sprang up — to see to my amazement a hooded head and a beard pressed to the glass.

"Goodness gracious! It's the man who let the caravan to me — and knocked Shadrack on the head!" I exclaimed. "I wouldn't have believed he'd have the nerve to show up here again. I'm glad you're with me, Micky. He's a dangerous character."

"Is that so? Well, I don't have any quarrel with him," Micky said hastily. "I'll be on my way."

"Oh, no! You must stand by me. Besides, it's probably he or his girl friend who stole your ring."

That suggestion halted Micky in his tracks. He stood just behind me as I opened the door.

"Hello, there!" The bearded, stocky figure was looking furtively from me to Micky. "Can I have a word with you, sister?"

"Make it brief, then," I requested, stooping to pick up Perkin, who was showing signs of being about to launch himself at the visitor. "After your behaviour yesterday, you've a nerve to approach

225

me again, haven't you? The police are supposed to be searching for you."

"Not for me. For the car."

"For you, too. You might have killed Mr Heston."

"Oh, that? Sorry about that, but I've no use for snoopers . . . and how was I to know who he was? I only meant to keep him out of the picture till we'd cleared the goods," he defended himself. "I was going to come back and turn him loose . . . but there was all that fuss and flap about Bessie . . . "

"You were smuggling stuff? Stolen goods?"

"Stolen? Hell, *no*! I'm not a thief," he protested indignantly. "That's what I've come to make clear to you. I borrowed your car, because I couldn't start my old bus. I didn't have any notion of pinching it. I want you to make that quite clear to those fools of cops. They buzzed me outside Weymouth when I was on my way back here, and dragged me off to make a statement."

"Oh?" I said weakly. "Where is my car?"

"Ask the police! They took it off me.

I told them you'd lent it to me. You'll back me up, won't you?"

The sheer audacity of the man left me virtually speechless. I stood there in the doorway, gaping at him. Seen by daylight, as I had supposed, he was swarthy and unprepossessing, with small, bright eyes under shaggy brows and a beak of a nose. Not really a thug, though, I surmised. He was trying to talk toughly, as he had talked on Saturday night, but it didn't ring quite true. He was probably some young fool who had been making money by smuggling, in a haphazard, amateurish fashion.

"I don't know why I should help you," I said coldly at last. "Who are you, anyway?"

"George Overton, if that means anything to you. My Pa owns Overton's Boat Yard, and I work for him. Mean as sin, he is, too. You can't blame me for using one of his boats to make a bit on the side," he announced defiantly.

"You took £50 off me under false pretences, stole my car, and knocked Mr Heston over the head," I accused him. "You're a menace."

227

"Oh, have a heart! I didn't mean him any harm . . . "

"And what about my diamond ring?" Micky had found his voice at last. "Are you going to swear you only borrowed that?"

"That cursed ring! That caused half the rumpus with Bessie." George Overton sounded positively indignant. "Fancy leaving a valuable ring around in a sponge-bag! Just asking for trouble, that was."

"You shouldn't have been ransacking my belongings," I pointed out sharply.

"That was Bessie. Jealous as a cat. Got it into her stupid head that I'd a girl friend on the q.t., and started nosing around," he said, still on an aggrieved note. "Well, Meg had been helping me with the boat, since Bessie had got herself in the family way and couldn't row, but I hadn't been keeping her here . . . "

"Presumably, Bessie and Meg were the two females who were screeching at each other, when Mr Heston turned up to investigate," I said, trying to make sense of his confused story.

"That's right! Proper mad, they were,

yelling and screaming, instead of getting on with the job and helping me to box up the watches," he said resentfully. "That was after Bessie had nosed round your caravan and found that cursed ring. Silly wench had tried it on for size and couldn't get it off again. 'Course, when Meg spotted the ring, she blew her top. Said if there were any diamonds on offer, she'd earnt them. She'd taken the risks. All Bessie had done was to put us on to the Camp. Bessie'd worked here in the shop, till August, and for a while we'd used her caravan."

"You seem to have landed yourself in a pretty thicket," Micky commented. "Where's my ring? That's what I want to know. I'm not concerned about your sordid affairs, but I want my ring back — *now*."

"Hell! It's on account of that blasted ring that Bessie bolted off like a mad thing. To pacify Meg, I explained where we'd found it, and Meg was threatening to tell the cops that Bessie had stolen it. It was the devil of a rumpus," George said feelingly. "You can't wonder that I lost my head and lashed out when that fellow came barging in on us."

"Can't you answer a straight question?" Micky was obviously bored by this recital of George's troubles. "Where is my diamond ring?"

"Still stuck on Bessie's finger, far as I know."

"Then, where's the girl, Bessie?" Micky demanded impatiently.

"That's what we're all asking. Her Dad got on to the cops when Bessie didn't come home last night. She just flung herself into her car and drove off — and I didn't see which way she went. I was trying to hush up Meg and finish packing the watches," George said sullenly. "Stop nagging about the damn' ring, will you? I've enough on my plate already . . . "

"Certainly, if you'd care to buy it off me. You can have it for £200, and that's a bargain price," Micky retorted coolly. "It must be worth at least £350."

"£200? See here, I'm not made of money . . . "

"You must have cleared quite a packet from your duty-free watches," Micky reminded him, smoothly, but with the faintest hint of a threat in his tone.

"I've heard that there are big profits to be made out of the smuggling racket, but I prefer to keep on the right side of the law."

I glanced from one man to the other, uncertain whether to be shocked or amused. George was disposed to bluster, but Micky was calmly inexorable. In the end, Micky consented to accept £175, cash down, and George, with glum reluctance, produced a fat roll of dirty looking fivers and counted out the money, as if it really hurt him to part with it.

"You don't know what it's like, being keen on a girl when your people don't approve, and your Dad doesn't pay you a living wage," he grumbled. "I never meant to land Bessie with a kid. I mean to say, I was trying to make a bit on the side, so that we could get married. With Meg, it was just business."

I felt sorry for both girls, but more especially for Bessie. Where was she? Lying helpless and unconscious somewhere? Were the police searching for her? Suppose she had staggered away and collapsed in the reed-bed somewhere?

Would I have seen or heard her? Surely, I must have done, during my frantic hunt for Perkin?

Of course, she had asked for trouble, in playing around with this man, George Overton, but who was I to censure her? Hadn't I teetered on the verge of falling for Micky Harris?

"I fancy this is where I bow out gracefully," Micky announced, pocketing the wad of fivers. "Sorry we couldn't make a going concern of it, Curly, but it was your choice."

13

"**Y**OUR choice — " and "your loss," Micky's tone added. It would always look that way to him, I didn't doubt. He would never undervalue himself and his assets.

"Goodbye, Micky!" I said flatly. "I hope the rescue operation is a success."

I didn't ask him not to leave me alone with George Overton. The man I'd thought of as 'that bearded thug' resembled a deflated balloon rather than a cornered rat.

In silence, we watched Micky glide across to a newish and obviously expensive, though exceedingly muddy sports car, which I recognised as belonging to Lettice. So — he had begun his campaign already, had he? Would he succeed in detaching Lettice from her chosen companions? Unless there was a perverse streak in her, she could scarcely prefer Foxy and Hal to Micky Harris. At least, that was my opinion. There was never any logic about personal tastes. I couldn't imagine how two girls could virtually have fought over stocky, bearded, unhandsome George Overton.

"Sharp, isn't he?" George said moodily, staring after the sports car. "Does himself well. What they call the Midas touch, eh?"

"That's not his car. It belongs to a friend. I suppose she lent it to him."

"She? Wish my girl friends were as well heeled. Meg rides a bike, and Bessie has only one of those old Beetles." He cleared his throat. "You will be a sport and tell the cops you let me borrow your car, won't you?"

"If that's what you've told them, I won't contradict you," I conceded. "You're obviously in enough trouble already. Not that you don't deserve to be — "

"I guess you've written me off as one of those no-good characters. Honestly, I'm worried sick about that damn' fool wench, Bessie," he said gruffly.

"I should think you have cause to be. Well, at any rate, the baby's all right."

"The *baby* ?" He started like a shying

horse. "What d'you mean? She's had the baby? How do you know?"

"It's quite a story. You'd better come in and sit down. I'll make some tea," I said resignedly.

My arms were beginning to ache from holding the wriggling Perkin. I seemed to have been standing in the doorway for hours, as if I were a she-bear, guarding my cub and den. Only, the cub wasn't mine, and neither was the den.

George Overton followed me into the sitting-room and gazed with awe at the sleeping babe.

"It's so tiny. Is it really alive? Really O.K.?" he asked, as if dumbfounded. "How come it's here and not with Bessie?"

When I had told him just how and where I had found the infant, a variety of expressions appeared in rapid succession on what was visible of his features above the growth of hair.

It was with an odd mixture of pride and sheepishness and gratification that he ejaculated: "That clearing! That was where we made love . . . the first time. It was the first time for Bessie, too. My

Mum was all wrong when she hinted that the girls who worked in the camp were easy lays. Bessie didn't even know enough to protect herself. Oh, hell, I hope she hasn't thrown herself into the sea!"

"Why would she have drowned herself?"

"She wasn't thinking straight. When Meg threatened to tell the cops that Bessie had pinched a diamond ring, Bessie panicked. She took off while Meg was helping me to truss up that snoopy pal of yours. She didn't know what she was doing."

"Distraught? Yes, she must have been, to abandon this poor mite."

I had an uneasy suspicion that Bessie might have been desperate enough to have hurled herself into the sea . . . but had she possessed the strength to plunge through the reed-bed and over the shingle to the water's edge? Wouldn't she have been likely to collapse halfway? And . . . where was her car? Shadrack, I was forced to admit, had had good reason for feeling concerned about her.

Did he know Bessie? Had he met her while she had been working in the shop? Had he subconsciously recognised her voice? Resolutely, I banished that uncomfortable surmise. George Overton was plainly convinced that he had been Bessie's first and probably her only lover — and he should know.

"You say the police are looking for Bessie?" I inquired, as I switched on the kettle. "We asked them last night to find this baby's mother, but they didn't appear to take us seriously."

"They're looking for her, but I wouldn't expect them to search the beach. They'll be keeping an eye open for her car, more likely," he said uneasily. "They weren't told about the row she had with Meg, or about the diamond ring. You can guess that I wasn't anxious to draw the cops' attention to the camp. I mean to say, they'd have wanted to know what we were doing here, without old Westcott's permission."

"Breaking and entering?"

"Well, no! Not really. Bessie had kept the key to the caravan she'd used while she was working here — and it happened to unlock several caravans of the same make. Fairer to say that we'd borrowed a caravan for the odd weekend or two."

"And wiser to pretend that it was for a romantic assignation, rather than as a smugglers' base."

He didn't rise to that. He was sitting slumped in an armchair, elbows on knees, chin in his hands. A foolish fellow, I thought, divided between exasperation and a reluctant pity. Men were unwise to embark upon crooked dealings, especially when they lacked the necessary nerve and reckless disregard of law and order to relish dodging the authorities. Foxy, for example, had obviously enjoyed raiding game preserves or doing a bit of shoplifting. He was 'foxy' by temperament. George Overton was more of a stag, but a faint-hearted stag, with inefficient antlers.

I made tea and handed him some, with milk and sugar, in one of the pottery coffee mugs.

He was sipping it gratefully when once again there came the sound of a car's engine and the scrunch of tyres on gravel.

"If that's the police — " George jerked in his chair. "Look, you will give me a break, won't you?"

"I'll keep quiet. Whether Mr Heston wishes to charge you or not with assaulting him, I can't tell you," I retorted.

"You could persuade him not to, couldn't you?"

The doorbell was pealing and the door itself was being smartly rapped. Perkin began to yap and the baby gave a preliminary squeal.

"Oh, blast! Here we go again," I said wearily. "Quiet, Perkin!"

I had barely slid back the lock when the door fairly burst open, almost sending me flying. This precipitate and unceremonious entrance was effected not by the police but — to my blank astonishment — by a large, tweed-clad, grey-cropped-haired, middle-aged lady. Behind gold-rimmed glasses, fierce grey eyes were glaring at me.

"Where is he? What have you done with him? Where's my grandson?" a strident voice demanded.

"What? Who?" I began, and was silenced by a groan from George.

"Mum! It's my Mum . . . "

"George!" The exclamation was one of profound relief. "So — that's where you are! I'm thankful to see that you have some sense of duty."

"Mum . . . Mum, what are you doing here?" George was on his feet, positively bleating. "Mum, it wasn't my fault . . . "

Piercing wails from the settee drowned his feeble bleats. The large lady swooped forward, and grabbed the baby.

"There, there, my precious! Come to Granny, then!" she cooed. "Keep that dog quiet, will you? It's frightening my grandson."

I caught up Perkin and stared helplessly at George. He was gasping, open-mouthed, like a netted flounder.

The large lady had seated herself firmly on the settee, and was rocking the baby vigorously. Too vigorously, I thought, but the little creature's wails died away into faint whimpers, as if in response to the purposeful handling.

"Bessie . . . " George got out with an effort.

"That poor child! Whatever were you thinking of to let her get herself into such a state?" his mother demanded. "If you'd only had the common-sense to come to me, I'd soon have fixed everything up for you both. Oh, no! Reckoned you could manage on your own, didn't you? All these modern ideas — free love, and one-parent families! I don't hold with 'em, as you should know."

"You didn't hold with Bessie," he reminded her in a feeble attempt at self-defence. "You ordered me to stop seeing her . . ."

"What has that to do with it? Didn't listen, did you? Selfish and inconsiderate as most men! Had your fun and left that poor child to pay for it. She might have died . . ."

"Bessie? She isn't dead?"

"No thanks to you!" Mrs Overton responded severely. "Tried to run her car into the sea. Can you believe it? Mercifully, the wheels got stuck in the shingle — and she collapsed in her seat. One of those long-line fishermen found her there, early this morning. Almost unconscious, poor child, and couldn't give any account of herself, so he made for the nearest call-box and rang 999."

"What happened?" I asked, as George

241

seemed to be struck speechless.

"You have to hand it to the police. They know their job. They whisked Bessie off to hospital and got in touch with her people. Her father rang me, blaming us for her suicide attempt. I went down to the hospital right away — " She tossed her grey-haired head arrogantly. "I soon put him in his place. I told him that, if he hadn't given the poor child a highly unsuitable stepmother, Bessie wouldn't have felt that desperate. I insisted on seeing Bessie — and she was sobbing her heart out over her lost baby. She'd made sure you'd follow her and rescue them both."

"I never even saw which way she went," George protested. "And how was I to guess that the baby was coming so soon?"

"No sense! Just out for your own selfish pleasures, like most men," she castigated him. "Of course, I went straight to the police to demand that they looked for the baby — and they told me at the Police Station that a baby had been found abandoned last night. So, naturally, I came straight on here."

"Naturally," I echoed, feeling as if I were encountering a tornado, guaranteed to sweep away every obstacle in its path.

"It wasn't likely I'd let that fool of a father of Bessie's and his made-up hussy of a wife take over my grandchild," Mrs Overton proclaimed. "As soon as Bessie's fit enough, you'll rush her straight to the Registrar's, George, and get yourselves properly married. D'you hear me? No more dilly-dallying. You've made your bed . . . "

"Yes, Mum. As you say . . . " George said weakly. Then, in a spurt of defiance, he added: "If Dad had paid me a decent wage, I'd have married Bessie months ago."

"We'll go into that in due course. In the meantime, our home is big enough to house the three of you," she assured him.

"Bessie won't like that, Mum."

"Bessie'll do as she's told."

Poor Bessie — and poor George! What chance would they stand against this very forceful mother of George's? I wondered compassionately. No doubt, she would be good to them, in her own fashion, but how much independence would she allow them? George would be forced eventually to break away and strike out for himself and his wife and child, if his marriage was to stand any hope of prospering. Couldn't his mother see that?

"I understand that it was this young woman who rescued the child. I hope you have thanked her adequately, George?" Mrs Overton turned to me with her purposeful air. "We're very much in your debt, my dear. If there's anything we can do, don't hesitate to call on us. Perhaps you would like to be put in touch with our solicitor?"

"Your solicitor?" I repeated blankly. "Why would I need a solicitor?"

"I understood that you were in some trouble with the police? Beryl Carter didn't give me any details, but she dropped a hint or two when she gave me this address." Mrs Overton rose, holding the baby possessively to her ample bosom. "I believe the police are on their way here. I hurried and took a short cut in order to forestall them. You can refuse to make a statement unless your solicitor is present, you know."

"I've nothing to conceal. I'm quite ready to make a statement. Thank you all the same, Mrs Overton."

"It doesn't do." She gave me a piercing glance. "Take my word for it. There's no such thing as free love — or as easy money, either. You have to pay for what you want, sooner or later."

"Yes," I said weakly. "I'm sure you're right. In actual fact, I haven't experienced either. I've been earning my living the hard way — as a children's nurse. At the moment, I'm on holiday."

I checked myself there. I didn't have to put up my defences against George's overpowering mother. She couldn't march *me* around for what she considered to be my ultimate good.

"I see!" she nodded. "I've nothing against Graham Westcott. I'm given to understand that he runs this Camp in a discreet and orderly fashion — but he is at least twice your age. Do you want to be treated as a child or a plaything?"

"Certainly not. I don't even know Mr Westcott . . . "

She wasn't listening. She went on in her

rapid manner: "You could come home with us and help with Baby . . . until Bessie's out of hospital. That would give you a breathing space . . . "

I couldn't imagine that anyone in her immediate vicinity had much of a chance to breathe freely. I thanked her politely and declined the offer.

She looked genuinely disappointed, as if frustrated in her attempt to pluck a brand from the burning, but George distracted her with an urgent: "Come on, then, Mum! We don't want more argy-bargy with the cops, do we? Let's try to keep a low profile."

"You'd better take Bessie's anorak, and the baby's bottle. The nappies, too . . . " Hastily I collected the baby's things and piled them into George's arms.

"Thanks! Thanks for everything," he said gruffly. "Er — you see the way it is?"

I saw — and yet, as I closed the door after them, I was almost envious of Bessie. I certainly wouldn't have wanted to be in her position, taken over by a domineering mother-in-law and not allowed to make any decisions for myself, but Bessie did have George and the baby . . .

To my dismay, tears began to well up in my eyes. I flopped back on the settee and gathered Perkin into my arms.

14

THE police arrived at mid-day; a middle-aged inspector in plain clothes, followed by a young constable, who was driving my car.

The Inspector was quiet, polite, and business-like. He asked a few pertinent questions, but gave no sign of whether he believed my answers or not. The constable took down my bald statement, which, apart from my assertion that I had lent my car to a friend — a Mr Michael Harris of The Down to Earth Community Centre — amounted to a series of negatives. No, I had not been in Malbury on Saturday. I had not visited High Rise, Malbury, since I had left Mrs Forrester's employment. I had not at any time, whilst employed by her, lent my latch-key or allowed it to pass out of my possession. I knew nothing about her jewellery. I had never handled any of it or even noticed it particularly. No, I certainly had not discussed the jewellery or its value with any friend of mine. No, I had not used my car until Saturday evening, when I had driven it here, from the community centre.

All negatives? Was I a negative and negligible character? I wondered unhappily. Was I losing out on life because I was chary of committing myself? Was I, unlike Mrs Overton's picture of me, too cautious ever to achieve anything worth-while?

'Nothing venture, nothing win'. Ought I to take that for my motto instead of 'Look before you leap'? How could I alter my whole nature? I simply wasn't capable of acting on impulse, unless I was confronted by an animal or a child in distress.

I had lent my car to a Mr Michael Harris, and subsequently to a Mr George Overton? The Inspector's tone was impersonal enough, but it contrived to convey the impression that I possessed a string of somewhat dubious men friends.

"Yes," I said flatly. "No law against lending a car, is there?"

"That could depend upon the purpose for which it was to be used," he answered blandly.

"Oh? Well, I've no idea why they wanted it. You'll have to ask *them* about that."

"We shall," he assured me.

Micky was highly unlikely to give himself away, if indeed he had anything to conceal. George Overton came into a different category, but, whatever the police prised out of him, I could scarcely be involved in it, I decided in relief.

Would I be remaining here or returning to the community centre? the Inspector wanted to know.

"I shall be staying here. I've hired a caravan till the end of the week," I told him.

"We understood that the camp had been closed . . . "

"It has, but Mr Heston has made an exception for me," I said, as calmly as I could.

"There was a question raised about obtaining money under false pretences." The inspector was referring to his notebook. "Did you wish to bring any charges against Mr Overton or Mr Heston?"

"Certainly not." Did that sound too emphatic? The constable was eyeing me speculatively. I added lamely: "I'm afraid there was a misunderstanding, but — er — it has been cleared up now."

The inspector looked up from his notebook, with no discernible expression on his inconspicuous features, but I could sense his rising impatience. I fancied that he would dearly love to shake me really hard. I seemed fated to have that unhappy effect on most men.

"On consideration, there is nothing you would like to add to your statement, Miss Melville?" he inquired, not exactly hopefully.

"I can't think of anything. When Mr Heston gets back here tonight, he may be able to tell you more . . ."

I had said 'when', but perhaps it should have been 'if'. What guarantee had I that Shadrack would return? Might not he have used the Malbury trip as an excuse to escape any further involvement with me?

After the police had taken their

departure, still outwardly polite but, I feared, inwardly dissatisfied and doubtful of me, horrid little misgivings wriggled their way into my mind. Why should I suppose that Shadrack was 'different'? What grounds had I for believing that he cared about me? For believing that the attraction between us wouldn't turn to exasperation on his part?

What on earth should I do if he returned from Malbury convinced that Samantha Tiggs and Millicent Forrester had given him a true account of Saturday's events? They couldn't, I reasoned desperately, prove that I had been in Malbury, but they might manage to convince Shadrack that I had been a willing accomplice to the theft.

He had said that he was a trained and experienced investigator, but Samantha could be very charming. Samantha had a way with men.

It was a wretched day, in more senses than one. I was wretched and so was the weather. Heavy rain started to fall in the early afternoon and showed no signs of slackening. I couldn't even take Perkin for a brisk walk.

I would have liked to prepare a really appetising evening meal against Shadrack's return, but the small deep-freeze was empty and switched off, and there was only butter and cheese, milk, bacon and eggs in the refrigerator.

I could have driven into Bridport or Weymouth for supplies, I realised belatedly, but I had virtually no cash left, and the banks would be closed. Idiot that I was, I should have headed straight for the nearest bank as soon as the police had departed. I should have cashed a cheque and gone on a shopping spree. I could have bought supplies and cooked a meal which would have demonstrated that I wasn't completely unversed in culinary skills.

Yes, but I might have made elaborate preparations and been left alone to eat the result. This was Monday. Shadrack might have gone back to his office — and thence to wherever he lived during his working week. This bungalow was merely his weekend refuge. Where did he live? Why hadn't I asked him? I didn't even know the name of his firm. If he chose to walk out on me, I wouldn't have any idea where to find him. Not that I would look for him, I assured myself firmly. I had never yet hunted or hounded a man. I couldn't begin now.

I made tea and toast. I played with Perkin. I fed him . . . and he went contentedly to sleep on my lap. The light was fading and the rain was still beating heavily against the windows. I couldn't remember ever having felt more inadequate or more forlorn.

I must have fallen into an uneasy doze when Perkin started up, yapping. I had barely registered the sound of the car's engine and the slam of a car's door before there was the welcome click of a latch-key in the lock. My heart began to thud.

A rush of cold, damp air, and the door closed again with a final-sounding click. Shadrack, a plastic shopping bag in each hand, came swiftly towards me, shaking water from his bare head.

"Shadrack! You're back!" I said inanely. "Oh, how wet you are!"

"It's raining hard — or hadn't you noticed?" He looked down at me with that familiar quirk of his brows. Then he smiled. "You look as if you've been asleep. All warm and pink and sweet."

As I was depositing Perkin on the floor and struggling to my feet, Shadrack bent over the armchair and dropped a kiss on my forehead. His skin felt cold and damp against mine, but his lips were warming. I reached up and hugged him. I couldn't help it. The relief was overwhelming. In a flash, all my misgivings scuttled away and I despised myself for ever having harboured them.

"That's nice! A nice welcome . . . " To my surprise, he looked absurdly gratified. "Just let me get rid of these bags . . . "

He deposited them on the table, stripped off his soaking anorak, and came back — to put both arms around me. This time, he kissed me full on the lips, and it was no merely friendly salutation.

"Someone to come home to has its points," he said, as if making a big concession. "Miss me?"

In view of that impulsive hug, I could scarcely deny it. I couldn't deny, either, that it was a singularly pleasant experience to be kissed by Shadrack. His lips on mine were neither too greedy and demanding nor too shy or too casual. A shade too possessive?

"Miss me?" he said again.

"Yes. Of course. And it's such a relief. That you aren't the police again," I said confusedly.

"The police would hardly use a latch-key."

I bit my lip. I foresaw that Shadrack would always rip through implausible or false excuses. Honest and straightforward himself, he demanded the same qualities from others. That might be disconcerting at times, but also a relief, because he was unlikely to hold candid answers against me.

"No," I agreed lamely. "I'm not thinking clearly . . . "

"Did the police give you a bad time? Poor darling!" His arms tightened around me. "Tired, worried, and hungry? I've bought steaks and tomatoes and peppers, crusty bread, and a bottle of good wine. I'll soon whip up a meal which will put new life into you."

"Thank you! That sounds marvellous . . . but you've done more than I have today. Let me do the cooking, while you change into dry clothes and towel your hair."

"Am I dripping over you? Sorry!"

He let go of me abruptly and I was conscious of an absurd pang of loss. There was no doubt about it. A man's arms did give one a lovely, warm, protected feeling. I had never owned and never would own a fur coat, because I couldn't bear the notion of wearing the pathetic little pelts of trapped or bred-for-slaughter animals, but I could imagine that furs could give a girl that same feeling of being warmed and cherished.

"The baby has gone?" Shadrack was glancing around the room. Was it my imagination or was he sniffing the air, dog-wise, as if to ascertain whether any strange males had visited his lair in his absence? "Did you induce the police to take her?"

"Oh, no! She was carried off by her grannie; her father's mother. It's quite a story — "

"Tell me! I'm all agog."

"Get yourself dry first."

"How wife-like that sounds!" He grinned at me. "We're not married yet,

257

my love, so don't order me around . . . "

"As if I would — or ever could! I just don't want you to catch cold," I blurted out confusedly.

"Protective, too? That's pleasant. Right, then, madam! You can heat up the grill while I change."

Had I made a mess of things — our relationship, to be precise — as usual? Had I antagonised him by my well-intentioned advice? I certainly hadn't meant to 'order him around', but I had been concerned about the soaking he seemed to have received. How could you help 'fussing' over people for whom you cared? Or was that an old-fashioned attitude?

When Shadrack emerged from his bedroom in dry clothes, his towelled hair standing up in comical little peaks, I said apologetically: "I didn't mean to fuss. I was just concerned about you. I've made some coffee to warm you."

"Splendid!" He came up behind me and patted me gently on the back. "I wasn't complaining. I was merely teasing you. It's good to have someone who cares. My last girlfriend, when I was in the throes of a really grim dose of 'flu, told me that I should 'get up and out in the fresh air instead of huddling over a hot water bottle in bed, as if I were a centurion.' She wasn't long on sympathy."

"Obviously not. A *centurion*?"

"That was near enough to centenarian for her."

"Oh?" There was a momentary silence as I poured out coffee for both of us. Then, although I knew it was unwise, I couldn't restrain myself from asking: "Was Bessie your last girl friend?"

"Bessie?" He looked blank. "Who's Bessie?"

"She worked in the camp shop this year. Until August."

"I rarely visit the site when the season is in full swing. There were several girl assistants. I didn't notice any of them in particular."

Was he being evasive? He had certainly looked blank rather than guilty when I had mentioned 'Bessie'.

"I just wondered. About the centurion girl," I said feebly.

"The centurion girl?" He flung back

his head in one of his spontaneous, whole-hearted laughs. "That's a grand name for her. She did expect to tell this man to 'go and he goeth', like the centurion in the New Testament . . . but she picked the wrong man in yours truly."

"Who was she?" I tried to speak lightly, but the twinkle in his eyes warned me that I hadn't succeeded.

"The Treasurer of our local Bird Watching Society, Alexandra Smith, and call her 'Sandy' at your peril. A young woman with a quite inflated notion of her own capabilities and attractions."

"Then, why — " I forced a smile. "Why did you pick such a forceful character for a girl friend?"

"I didn't. She picked me. She marched me around for several weeks. I was trying to escape, without inflicting any serious damage to her *amour propre*, when mercifully I went down with 'flu." He sipped the hot coffee appreciatively. "Amongst other things we have in common, Helen love, is a reluctance to hurt people. Also, the form of diffidence which makes us rather absurdly grateful to anyone who appears to like us."

"Oh, Shadrack! Is it like that for you, too? I didn't suppose it ever was for a man."

"My sweet Helen, you've a lot to learn. I don't believe you've any idea of your own assets . . . including the all-too-rare ability to make really good coffee," he answered, holding out his mug for a refill. "Your ears should have been burning from all that was said about you at High Rise."

"Oh? About my temper, do you mean? Caroline was dreadfully provoking," I said defensively. "I know I shouldn't have spanked her, but she was behaving insufferably."

"I don't doubt it! A week of Miss Caroline was enough for her Mamma, who evidently lacks your patience. As from today, that spoilt brat has become a weekly boarder at her school, and her mother is beseeching you to reconsider your decision and return to look after the other two small girls who, incidentally, appear quite devoted to you."

"Reconsider? Return?" I echoed weakly. "Mrs Forrester sent me packing. I would have expected her to have a replacement by now."

"It seems that the Head of the Agency, for which you have been working, greeted Mrs Forrester's request for a replacement somewhat frigidly. She insisted that, if one of their most competent and satisfactory nurses had found the children too hard to handle, the Agency would prefer not to retain Mrs Forrester as a client."

"Goodness gracious!" I gasped. "I was ticked off for losing my temper. The Head didn't give me any indication that she would support me."

"Discipline must be maintained? Rules must be respected?" Shadrack nodded. "Anyway, Mrs Forrester and the little girls are excessively anxious to have you back again."

"But . . . she thought I had stolen her jewellery," I said dazedly. "She told the police so."

"The grill's ready now. I hope you like black pepper and garlic salt on your steak?" Shadrack put down his empty mug and opened the small store cupboard with a purposeful air.

"Yes. Yes, I do!" I responded absently. "Shadrack, don't tantalise me! Did you find out anything about the missing jewels?"

"Of course. I told you I was a skilled interrogator and investigator. It was a simple matter to induce the little girls to tell me all they knew. Then, I visited Samantha Tiggs. She attempted to plead ignorance, but, reminded that perjury was a serious offence, she 'came clean', as she herself expressed it."

I had to contain my impatience whilst he sprinkled liberal helpings of black pepper and garlic salt over the juicy looking steaks and arranged them under the grill. Then he found a sharp knife and sliced up the peppers and tomatoes.

15

SHADRACK'S eyes were twinkling behind his glasses when at last he resumed his narrative.

"Maddening of me to keep you waiting," he grinned. "I was just testing you for the explosion point. Full marks, my love! Well now, to go back to Samantha. It seems that she had been baby-sitting on her free evenings, and she had put it into the little girls' heads that, if they plagued their mother sufficiently, she might send for you to come back to them."

"How odd! I mean, surely Samantha didn't want me to come back?" I said doubtfully.

"Oh, no! Her scheme went much deeper. She's pretending now that it was young Diana's idea to tease Mrs Forrester by hiding her jewels, but in fact I'm fairly sure Samantha and her boy-friend had planned to dispose of them, as soon as the hue and cry had subsided," Shadrack said grimly. "Sydney Fane called at High Rise on Saturday afternoon, ostensibly to see Samantha and make a date with her. Diana was easily persuaded to hand the jewels over to him 'to hide'. Apparently, it didn't occur to Mrs Forrester to question the children. They were supposed to have been in the park with Samantha when the theft took place."

I drew a deep breath. I looked at him admiringly.

"However did you guess? And how did you persuade Diana to talk? She's a bright child but she's nervous of strangers, particularly of men."

"I'm quite good with children, new-born babies excepted," he assured me. "Mrs Forrester was very reluctant to allow me to interview Diana and Sara, but I insisted. I pointed out that I was less alarming than a policeman would be."

"Clever of you — " I said appreciatively. "Even cleverer to have extracted the truth from Samantha. How did you manage it?"

"I had the advantage of knowing in advance that she was lying about your car. Liars will try to be too plausible. If she hadn't added that fancy touch about your car's having been parked on the double yellow lines, she might have sounded convincing. As it was, you had seized immediately on that weak spot in her story. No professional crook would be idiot enough to leave his get-away car just where it was bound to catch the eye of a traffic warden or a passing police car."

"She didn't see my car at all, did she?"

"No. She didn't. That was simply a piece of feminine spite. As I'd suspected, she was furious with you for having annexed Micky Harris." Shadrack turned the sizzling steaks deftly and then, once more, appeared to be sniffing the air for an intruder. "Has that fellow been pestering you again?"

"Not exactly. He came here for his diamond ring. I've had quite a day. Baby's father was here, too."

"What? *Who?* What happened?"

"Shall we wait until I've laid the table and the steaks are ready?" I suggested sweetly. "It's quite a long story."

He gave me a quick, exasperated

glance. Then he laughed.

"Tit for tat? Right! I'm glad you have spirit, Helen love. I don't like meek, martyr types. Mind you always stand up to me!"

"Oh! Wouldn't you find that irritating?"

"Why?"

"I don't know. Men do seem to find me rather exasperating."

"Much better to be exasperated than bored. Not to worry! I fancy we shall quickly discover how to handle each other," he said calmly. "Do you like grapes and pears? When I was in the greengrocer's, I suddenly thought how ridiculous it was, to be contemplating spending the rest of my life with a girl, and yet not to know if she liked garlic or grapes or pears."

Again I drew a deep breath.

"The rest of your life?" I repeated dazedly.

"Well, yes! I'm one of the old-fashioned kind, who believes that marriage is for keeps. That's why I've remained unattached. I had to be sure."

"You can't possibly be sure of me. It's much too soon."

"Don't panic, my love! I wasn't proposing to rush you to the altar immediately. From what I've learnt of you, I surmise that you'll answer Millicent Forrester's S.O.S.?"

"I'd like to, yes. It seemed so untidy and unsatisfactory, to be sent off as I was. I would like to finish my stint there . . . only there's Perkin. I can't abandon him."

He nodded approvingly.

"I warned Mrs Forrester about the pup. She said you would be welcomed back on any terms, and the children would be delighted to have a dog in the house. I also warned her that you wouldn't be staying on indefinitely; that you would probably be getting married early in the New Year, if not before."

"In the New Year?" I echoed in relief.

"I can come down to Malbury at weekends. I have to give you a fair chance to find out the worst about me," he said easily. "I can be patient . . . and I fancy that courting you will be most pleasant and rewarding."

"I hope so . . . " I felt as though I were being swept along in an increasingly strong current. "There is a lot about *you* I don't understand. Why you were so deeply concerned about Bessie, for instance?"

"*Bessie?*" he said again, perplexedly. "I don't recall this Bessie . . . "

"The baby's mother. You were fearfully worried about her," I reminded him.

"Certainly, I was worried about the baby's mother, but I had no idea of her identity." He was silent for a moment or two, his thin features wearing a grim, withdrawn expression. Then he straightened himself and said flatly: "I was thinking of my own mother. Before I was born, my parents were living in a picturesque but isolated and somewhat primitive country cottage. My father was working late most nights. He wasn't, as I've already told you, a good business man. He was always in arrears and in a muddle with his book-keeping."

He paused. I didn't speak. I could feel it in my bones that this was a story he found painful to recall. He was forcing himself to tell it, because it was something he wanted me to know. Somehow, the very evenness of his tone was expressive of his tightly reined-in emotion; or at least it was to me. I knew that my own voice took on that same flatness when I was trying not to show that I was hurt.

"She didn't like being left alone after dark, but she wasn't a clinger. She didn't complain. That's what my aunt — her sister — told me years later," Shadrack went on again. "According to my aunt, my mother was 'too brave for her own good; too proud ever to ask for help'. Anyway, Mother was alone in the cottage on the evening when the birth pains began. It was a Monday evening, after a very stormy weekend, in which gales had brought down most of the telephone lines in the village, including my parents'. So — there she was, with no telephone or car, no near neighbours, and, of course, no electricity."

"Grim," I said feelingly, as he paused again.

"Grim," he echoed. "Nobody knows exactly what happened. Did she light the portable oil stove because she was chilly? Did it flare up at her and catch her clothing on fire? Or did she turn faint, fall against the stove, and overturn it?"

"Oh! Oh, *no* — " I was shuddering; horror-stricken. "There was a fire?"

"A neighbouring farmer, bringing in a newly calved cow and her calf from the fields, saw the blaze. His telephone was out of order, too, but he sent his son in search of a 'phone to ring up the Fire Brigade. He himself and his wife came straight over in their Land-Rover. They found my mother badly burned and unconscious, lying in a cabbage-patch just outside the back-door. She must have crushed out the flames on her clothes by throwing herself on to the earth, among the soaking wet cabbages."

"Oh, Shadrack! How ghastly! So — that's why — "

"I was named 'Shadrack.' Precisely," he said sombrely. "The cottage was a fiery furnace beyond saving. The farmer and his wife lifted my mother into the Land-Rover and drove her off to the nearest hospital. I was born five minutes after they'd carried my mother into the delivery room. I, as you see, survived that ghastly night. She didn't."

There was nothing I could say. I just reached out and put my arms around him. For a moment or two we stood there, close together, in silence. Then, he stirred.

He dropped a kiss on my forehead, and said: "Bless you, my love! We won't talk of it again. It was a long time ago. You can be thankful that I wasn't named 'Cabbage', or 'Rover', or even 'Percy', after the good neighbour who rescued us."

"I like 'Shadrack'. It's uncommon, and it suits you."

"Well, you understand now why I was concerned about that baby's mother? She might have been lying in the reed-bed, unconscious."

"Yes, of course. Actually, she had collapsed in her car, but she is going to be all right."

"That's a mercy." He gave me a searching glance.

"Were you really afraid I had been involved with that young woman?"

"No, not really. I just wondered," I said lamely.

"Would you have cared if I had been?"

272

"I should have been sorry, yes. It would have been tough on you, because obviously she was keen on George, the baby's papa."

"Not on your own account?"

"Why should it have meant anything to me?"

"Why, indeed? And why should I feel madly jealous of your friend, Micky?"

"Oh, no! You couldn't be. You wouldn't have any cause."

"That's a relief! If you're sure? Probably, you mean far more to him than you've realised. You persistently underestimate yourself," he chided me. "In a less candid character, that could be called mock modesty."

"I think the steaks are just about ready," I said hurriedly. "And I haven't laid the table . . . "

"Helen, the elusive? Oh, well, 'man is the hunter, woman is his game', so we're told — and I prefer it that way! What about you?"

"Have you warmed the plates?" I inquired, busying myself at the table. "Now, what else do we need? Bread? Did you say you'd bought some fresh bread?"

"A crusty French loaf."

"Marvellous! I've suddenly discovered that I'm ravenously hungry."

It was a simple meal and yet one of the most delicious I could ever remember. Rain was still lashing against the windows, but I was filled with a warm sense of well-being. I was daring to believe that Shadrack was right and that we could have a future together once we 'had learnt to handle each other'.

In between mouthfuls of the juicy, tasty steak, I satisfied his curiosity about my day. He was eager for every detail of Micky's and George's visits. We laughed together over Micky's bargaining, and I managed to enlist Shadrack's sympathy on George's behalf.

George certainly deserved some form of retribution, we agreed, but it had evidently overtaken him without any spurring from us. Between his parents and Bessie, he had got himself well and truly hog-tied.

"He'll find compensations, though. One may shrink from ultra-possessiveness, but it's good to have someone who cares," Shadrack said meditatively. "George may be luckier than he knows."

"Haven't you any family, apart from your uncle? What about the aunt you mentioned?"

"She married an Australian fruit farmer. I hear from her at Christmas and on my birthday, but it's rarely indeed that she takes a trip over here."

"I'm sorry . . . "

"Uncle Graham's a good chap, but he's very much the business man. Hasn't 'time for sentiment or socialising', as he puts it. His wife is one of those ardent committee women, active in various charitable and fund-raising enterprises. They haven't any family," Shadrack said matter-of-factly. "They've been kind to me after their fashion, but Uncle sometimes makes me feel that I'm one of his investments, and Aunt that I'm one of her good causes."

I smiled, as I sensed he meant me to, because he wasn't the man to solicit sympathy, but my heart ached for the loneliness he must have endured since his father's death. Everyone, however self-sufficient, needed someone who cared.

"I've been lucky — except that I have often longed for a brother or sister.

My father has always been marvellously understanding," I said with gratitude for my home background. "My mother's a grand person, but not exactly motherly. She's a G.P., and usually rushed off her feet, but she seems to thrive on it."

"Will I pass muster, do you suppose?" he asked diffidently.

"Oh, certainly! Without any doubt whatsoever. But . . . " I hesitated, and he gave me one of his heart-warming smiles.

"No cause for alarm. I'm not trying to tamper with your brakes, love. We'll proceed at your own speed, provided you'll keep the lights on green."

"Oh, yes! They'll stay on green," I promised, supremely thankful for his perception. "I'd like to finish my stint with Mrs Forrester, but I always go home for Christmas. My parents count on me."

"I can imagine it."

"Can you? My mother says Christmas for her means a rapid succession of babies, burns and broken limbs. My father's hard at it with Carol and Christmas Services, weddings and baptisms. So . . . I

276

organise our family Christmas . . . a real old-fashioned Christmas . . . "

"Yes?"

"I make the Christmas pudding and mince pies. I forage in the woods for holly and evergreens. I decorate the Vicarage and help to decorate the Church. I go out with the carol singers and help with the Sunday School children's party," I said breathlessly. "It's all very simple . . . and some people might find it boring . . . but I love it. And, Shadrack — "

"Yes?" he said again, encouragingly. "It sounds grand to me."

"I was just wondering if you would care to come home with me this Christmas? You would be warmly welcomed," I got out with an effort. Did that sound too formal? "I mean, I'd love you to come . . . "

"Thank you, my love! I would like that. I would like it very much indeed."

His tone was quiet, but he was smiling and, as our eyes met, his told me all I needed to know. This was no passing attraction. This was for keeps. I had found my someone who cared . . .

TO FIGHT THE WILD
Rod Ansell and Rachel Percy

Lost in uncharted Australian bush, Rod Ansell survived by hunting and trapping wild animals, improvising shelter and using all the bushman's skills he knew.

COROMANDEL
Pat Barr

India in the 1830s is a hot, uncomfortable place, where the East India Company still rules. Amelia and her new husband find themselves caught up in the animosities which seethe between the old order and the new.

THE SMALL PARTY
Lillian Beckwith

A frightening journey to safety begins for Ruth and her small party as their island is caught up in the dangers of armed insurrection.

THE WILDERNESS WALK
Sheila Bishop

Stifling unpleasant memories of a misbegotten romance in Cleave with Lord Francis Aubrey, Lavinia goes on holiday there with her sister. The two women are thrust into a romantic intrigue involving none other than Lord Francis.

THE RELUCTANT GUEST
Rosalind Brett

Ann Calvert went to spend a month on a South African farm with Theo Borland and his sister. They both proved to be different from her first idea of them, and there was Storr Peterson — the most disturbing man she had ever met.

ONE ENCHANTED SUMMER
Anne Tedlock Brooks

A tale of mystery and romance and a girl who found both during one enchanted summer.

CLOUD OVER MALVERTON
Nancy Buckingham

Dulcie soon realises that something is seriously wrong at Malverton, and when violence strikes she is horrified to find herself under suspicion of murder.

AFTER THOUGHTS
Max Bygraves

The Cockney entertainer tells stories of his East End childhood, of his RAF days, and his post-war showbusiness successes and friendships with fellow comedians.

MOONLIGHT
AND MARCH ROSES
D. Y. Cameron

Lynn's search to trace a missing girl takes her to Spain, where she meets Clive Hendon. While untangling the situation, she untangles her emotions and decides on her own future.